# HONORS FOR APRIL HENRY

Edgar Award Finalist

Anthony Award Winner

ALA Best Books for Young Adults

ALA Quick Picks for Young Adults

Barnes & Noble Top Teen Pick

Winner of the Maryland Black-Eyed Susan Book Award

Missouri Truman Readers Award Selection

TLA TAYSHAS Selection

New York State Reading Association Charlotte
Award Winner

Oregon Council of Teachers of English Spirit Book
Award Winner

One Book for Nebraska Teens

Golden Sower Honor Book

YALSA Quick Pick for Reluctant Young Adult Readers

# PLAYING WITH

# WITH

# FIRE

## OTHER MYSTERIES BY APRIL HENRY

*Girl, Stolen*

*The Night She Disappeared*

*The Girl Who Was Supposed to Die*

*The Girl I Used to Be*

*Count All Her Bones*

*The Lonely Dead*

*Run, Hide, Fight Back*

*The Girl in the White Van*

## THE POINT LAST SEEN SERIES

*The Body in the Woods*

*Blood Will Tell*

# PLAYING WITH FIRE

## FIRE

**APRIL HENRY**

*Christy Ottaviano Books*

HENRY HOLT AND COMPANY

NEW YORK

Henry Holt and Company, *Publishers since 1866*
Henry Holt® is a registered trademark of Macmillan Publishing Group, LLC
120 Broadway, New York, NY 10271 • fiercereads.com

Our books may be purchased for business or promotional use. For information on bulk purchases, please contact your local bookseller or the Macmillan Corporate and Premium Sales Department at (800) 221-7945 x5442 or by email at specialmarkets@macmillan.com.

Library of Congress Cataloging-in-Publication Data
Names: Henry, April, author.
Title: Playing with fire / April Henry.
Description: First edition. | New York : Henry Holt and Company, 2021. | Christy Ottaviano books. | Audience: Ages 12–18. | Audience: Grades 7–9. | Summary: "When a fire engulfs an Oregon forest, a group of trapped hikers must find another way out"— Provided by publisher.
Identifiers: LCCN 2020020572 | ISBN 9781250234063 (hardcover)
Subjects: CYAC: Survival—Fiction. | Forest fires—Fiction. | Wilderness areas—Fiction. | Hiking—Fiction.
Classification: LCC PZ7.H39356 Pl 2021 | DDC [Fic]—dc23
LC record available at https://lccn.loc.gov/2020020572

First Edition, 2021

Book design by Mike Burroughs

Printed in the United States of America by LSC Communications, Harrisonburg, Virginia

10  9  8  7  6  5  4  3  2  1

*For Randy, who has loved the woods*
*even longer than he has loved me*

## CHAPTER 1

# BLANKET OF FIRE

6:22 P.M.

**WHEN JASON AND BRIAN** had scouted this stretch of road in the middle of the week, it had been empty. But now, early on a Saturday evening, Jason counted a half-dozen parked cars. The lot for the nearby trail to Basin Falls must be full.

Only Brian's plan had called for parking here, and he had made it clear that Jason shouldn't deviate from the plan. And so far, Brian's plan was going like clockwork.

So Jason found a spot. Before he got out, he cranked down the windows. Then he opened up the back of the little 1984 Chevette he had bought off Craigslist. Four hundred cash. Three hundred for the car, and another hundred for not asking questions. Later, Jason had destroyed the burner phone he'd used to arrange the deal.

The trunk of the hatchback was empty except for a single road flare.

After he retrieved it, Jason looked up and down the road but didn't see anyone. He walked around the car until it was between him and the road. He pulled the lid off the white cap to expose the coarse red striking surface. Then he twisted off the cap. He took a slow breath, trying to steady his nerves. Then in a single fast movement, he struck the black button on the end of the flare across the coarse red surface on the plastic cap, like striking a giant match. It lit with a hiss and a shower of sparks, reminding him of fireworks.

He tossed it into the back seat, the way Brian had said.

And now he was supposed to walk away. Walk back down the road to where it joined up with the bigger road. Brian would pick him up. And meanwhile, their getaway car would turn into a fireball, destroying any prints and DNA they had left.

But what if the flare guttered and went out?

A flame started on the stained fabric of the seat, then began to inch up the back. It felt like magic. He had just created it out of nothing. Now it danced and moved like a living thing. The flames were yellow in the center, then orange and finally red at the edges.

Smoke was beginning to billow out of the car. A breeze blew through the driver's side window and pushed the flames toward the middle of the seat.

The smoke was turning from gray to black. It tasted acrid. Jason stepped back, coughing, still reluctant to walk away. What if someone showed up with a fire extinguisher and put it out?

The flames reached out of the car, up past the roof. Inside, the headliner caught. It fell, a blanket of fire.

*Boom!* The back glass of the hatchback shattered, and a piece of metal shot toward him. It landed in the dry weeds, and suddenly they were on fire as well. Suddenly, everything was on fire.

Jason turned and ran, trying to get ahead of the flames.

# The Seattle Public Library

West Seattle Branch

www.spl.org

Checked Out On: 3/24/2022 17:25
XXXXXXXXXXXX7805

| Item Title | Due Date |
| --- | --- |
| 0010104585152 | 4/7/2022 |

0010 0002000 1

Playing with fire

0010103658869                          4/14/2022

You'd be home now

0010094092748                          4/14/2022

This is not a love letter

# of Items: 5

Renew items at www.spl.org/MyAccount
or 206-386-4190

Sign up for due date reminders
at www.spl.org/notifications

## CHAPTER 2

# RIBBON OF SCAR

### 6:24 P.M.

**A FLAT *POP* SPLIT** the hot summer air. It sounded far away but also out of place.

Natalia heard it even over the rush of the waterfall. She lifted her head from the beach towel they had spread on a wide flat boulder. "What was that?"

Next to her, Wyatt, who had been half-asleep, pushed himself up on his elbows. His eyebrows pulled together. "It almost sounded like a rifle shot."

"But it's not hunting season, right?" Natalia was pretty sure hunting season was in the fall. Not in the middle of a scorching August.

"No. It's not." Wyatt was still listening, head tilted, hazel eyes narrowed. But the sound wasn't repeated.

Had anyone else heard it? A couple of hikers still at Basin Falls were also staring toward the trail that led back to the parking lot, less than two miles away. But most seemed to have noticed nothing. A pitted-out plump guy in his late twenties was drinking a Gatorade on the sun-warmed rocks. A college-age girl was taking a selfie with the falls in the background, while her boyfriend threw a stick for his medium-sized brown dog. Thirty feet from them, a mom and dad were putting their toddler into a backpack-like contraption.

Wyatt finally relaxed. "Sounds can carry weird out here." He shrugged. "What time is it, anyway?"

Natalia checked her phone. "Six twenty-five." Even though the corner of the display had shown the same thing since they left the parking lot to start the hike here, it was still disconcerting to see zero bars and the words "No Service."

"Oops. I must have drifted off." Wyatt picked up his socks. "We should get going. Even though it's an easy trail, we don't want to be on it after dark."

Natalia didn't think it had been all that easy, what with the roots and rocks and being uphill. Sunset was still nearly two hours away, but it had taken them almost an hour to hike here.

Wyatt reached for his hiking boots, scuffed with use. She did the same, wishing she didn't have to put hers back on. They were so hot and heavy, and because they were brand-new, they had already left a red spot on one toe.

And had she really needed them? Some people had made it here in Tevas. The girl taking a selfie was actually wearing flip-flops. Natalia had considered this a trip to the wilderness and prepared accordingly. Maybe it had been overkill to buy the hiking boots and the emergency supplies. It had certainly been expensive, way more than she'd expected.

After Natalia finished tying her boots, Wyatt pulled her to her feet. Although they had spent hours next to each other this summer, it was the first time they had

4

deliberately touched. She was aware of his slightly calloused palm, his strong fingers, but he released her hand as soon as she was up.

Natalia couldn't quite figure Wyatt out. She thought he liked her, but today he'd treated her just like a friend. Which was what they had become at the Dairy Barn this summer. Coworkers and friends. Handing out samples on tiny blue plastic spoons. Joking as they packed ice cream into cones. Bumping hips in the small space behind the counter.

And then last week Wyatt had found out that Natalia had never been hiking.

"What? Never? This is Portland!" He widened his eyes dramatically. "The place where babies are born wearing Gore-Tex and hiking boots. People come from all over the world to hike the Columbia Gorge. You live less than an hour away, and you've managed to go seventeen years without even taking a day hike?"

"Sorry." With a half smile, she hung her head, savoring his attention.

"What about Outdoor School?" In Portland, most fifth graders attended Outdoor School, where they stayed in cabins, tramped around in the woods, and learned about nature.

"I was sick that week." That was one way of putting it. Natalia had been in a hospital, sedated. "And my parents aren't really the outdoor-adventure type."

"We're going to have to fix that," Wyatt had said.

Which was why they were now scrambling up the hill and back to the trail. Natalia took one last look at the falls.

She had to admit they were beautiful. White water poured over the lip of the basin to splash thirty feet into what nature and time had turned into a natural swimming hole. The rush of water was nearly hypnotic.

They reached the trail. It had been carved into the side of a valley that sloped down to a creek. Above them, evergreens stretched to the sky. The slanted hillside was carpeted with ferns and other small green plants. The space felt immense, big and open, capped only by the bright blue sky.

The way back was mostly downhill. Natalia had been looking forward to it, thinking it would be easier, but momentum actually seemed to be working against her. She felt off-balance. With each step, her ankles wobbled and her knees protested.

And then she stepped on a loose rock. Her right foot started to slip. As her arms pinwheeled, her stomach crammed into the back of her throat.

Natalia lurched to the right. Toward the creek. For a split second, she saw how it would all end, with her body tumbling down the steep slope to rest broken and bloody by the water far below.

Then Wyatt caught her wrist and pulled her back. "Whoa there!"

"I thought going downhill would be easier!" She was gasping.

"It seems like it should be, doesn't it?" He gave her a sympathetic grin. "The trick is to keep your knees bent and take short steps. Try to keep your weight centered—don't lean forward or back."

They started off again. Natalia's steps were now so short they were more of a shuffle. Whenever Wyatt realized she had fallen behind, he stopped and waited patiently. His gray T-shirt didn't even look wet under the arms.

All of Natalia's skin was slick. Sweat was actually dripping off the ends of her hair. She couldn't wait to get home and jump into the shower. Maybe her parents were right. They thought being trapped in the middle of the woods without electricity, running water, or a car was reserved for survivors of the apocalypse or at least a plane crash. Certainly not something anyone with sense would *choose*.

Coming up the trail toward them was a dark-haired white guy in his thirties. He wore a black ball cap, dark cargo pants, and a black T-shirt that showed off his muscles and a long fresh scratch on one arm. He glanced back over his shoulder a couple of times, but the path behind him was empty.

Earlier, Wyatt had told Natalia that trail etiquette dictated whoever was going uphill had the right of way, so she stepped aside.

The other guy was moving fast, nearly jogging. Even though he was getting a late start, at his pace he would still have time to make it to the falls, admire them, and then turn around and beat Wyatt and Natalia back. As he passed, he gave them a nod, his eyes hidden by sunglasses. In one hand was what looked like the top to a bottle, but his other hand was empty.

When Natalia caught up with Wyatt for what seemed like the thousandth time, a scent tickled her nose. She stopped in her tracks. Smoke, but not from a cigarette. It smelled like a campfire. "Do you smell that?"

Wyatt sniffed the air. "The Cougar Creek fire's still burning."

At the word *fire*, a sour taste spread across Natalia's tongue. Memories crowded into her thoughts, but she pushed them away. "There's a fire?"

"It's been burning for a couple of weeks. It's about seventy percent contained. Didn't you see the helicopters carrying those gigantic buckets of flame retardant when we were driving here?"

"I saw them but I guess I didn't think about what they were for."

"We're in the middle of a drought." Wyatt's mouth twisted. "That's why I was worried that sound might have been a rifle shot. A lot of people go shooting in the Gorge, and some of them aren't that careful. But these woods are tinder-dry. If they use exploding targets or a bullet sparked against a rock, it could cause a fire."

Despite the heat, Natalia shivered. Her hand went to the back of one pant leg. Through the cloth, her fingers traced the ribbon of scar on her left thigh. Trying to reassure herself, she said. "But it's so green." She waved a hand to indicate the dark evergreens, the brighter green ferns and plants.

"All this green can turn into fuel if the conditions are right." He saw her expression. "Don't worry. We're almost back to the car. And that fire is several miles away."

They kept walking down the trail, their boots thudding softly. Her stomach growled, despite the sandwiches they had eaten only an hour ago. Maybe they could stop at a drive-through on their way back to Portland.

Focused on her feet, she almost ran into Wyatt's back. He had stopped short. His head was up, and when she stepped to the side to look at his face, his eyes were wide.

"What's the matter?" Everything looked just the way it had before. Then Natalia realized it wasn't what Wyatt was seeing. It was what he was *hearing*.

A rumbling.

"What *is* that?"

Instead of answering, he broke into a jog, disappearing around a turn in the path. More slowly, Natalia followed. The air was starting to look cloudy. Misty.

When she rounded the corner, she felt the heat on her skin. Now smoke was everywhere.

Natalia blinked, as if it were a mirage, but what she saw didn't go away.

Several hundred yards ahead, the woods were on fire. The woods they needed to go through.

## CHAPTER 3

# TRUE BUT NOT THE TRUTH

6:59 P.M.

**NATALIA PUT HER HAND** over her mouth. The fire moved like a living thing, like a dancer, like water, like a torn and fluttering flag. It crackled and snapped as it crisped and then consumed ferns and wildflowers and plants she didn't know the names of.

It wasn't a solid wall of flame. Some spots were still green, while in others the fire was thick, flaring up as it found new fuel, filling the air with pale smoke. The flickering orange and yellow was a sharp contrast to the bright green ground cover. The flames were nibbling on the trunks of some of the small trees that bordered the trail but hadn't leapt into the canopies. Yet.

Natalia's throat was tight, her breathing shallow. For the past six years, she had avoided even the smallest of fires. Matches. Lighters. Birthday candles. Smoldering incense. And of course bigger things like firepits and fireplaces.

Now her nightmares had come to life.

Slowly, she became aware Wyatt was repeating her name. "Natalia. Natalia, are you okay?"

She was not okay. She was back to being eleven years old, gasping in the smoke.

"I'm afraid of fire."

In her mind, she was again crawling across the flat tan carpet, coughing and gagging.

Wyatt put his hand under her chin, turning her head so she was facing him and not the flames. At first she resisted, the muscles in her neck rigid, before yielding to the gentle pressure of his fingers. Their eyes locked. This time when he grabbed her hand, he squeezed and didn't let go.

"Listen to me. We're going to be okay. But we can't stay here. We're going to go back to the falls. It's got that rocky beach with no trees nearby. And all that water. We'll be safe there."

"But what about the fire?"

He surveyed the flames with narrowed eyes. "It's not that far from the parking lot. Someone's probably already called 9-1-1. If the Forest Service could divert a single helicopter with one of those giant buckets of fire retardant, they could nip this thing in the bud."

But what if they didn't know about the fire? Natalia checked her phone, but it still read "No Service."

As she slid it back into her pocket, Wyatt said, "I think if I climbed up above the falls I might be able to get a bar or two." He tugged her hand. "Come on, let's go back."

When they hurried around the bend, the couple with the toddler was coming toward them. The parents were slender, Asian American, maybe in their late thirties. The child had both his hands fisted in his father's black hair. Looking at him, the smell of smoke in her nostrils, Natalia felt faint and far away, as if she were observing herself from above.

Wyatt stepped into the middle of the path. "You can't go back this way. There's a fire, and it's cut off the trail. I think we should all just go back to the falls."

The dad scowled. "What are you talking about? Are you joking?"

Wyatt raised his empty hands. "Why would we joke about that? Look at all the smoke in the air. The fire's just a few hundred yards up the trail."

"And Trask is really tired." The mom shook her head. She had a spiky black haircut.

"We just came through there like an hour ago and there wasn't any fire," the dad said. "Maybe we could still get through."

Wyatt shook his head. "It's moving pretty fast."

But it was like the couple hadn't heard him. Without another word, the man walked past them. When the edge of the child carrier knocked against Natalia, he didn't apologize. More slowly, the woman followed.

Natalia exchanged a look with Wyatt. "Maybe we should go after them?"

"They'll figure it out in a minute."

"But what about their kid?" The memory of her little brother swamped her. To steady herself, she rested her palm on the rough bark of a tree trunk. Her therapist, Dr. Paris, called it anchoring to the real world.

"I'm sure they won't really risk it once they see it. They just need to wrap their heads around reality."

Natalia and Wyatt started back up the hill. It was an effort to keep lifting her boots. They had worked until two thirty and then driven the hour out here. At least now that she couldn't see the fire, her fear wasn't as paralyzing. The authorities were probably already redirecting one of those helicopters. Maybe she and Wyatt would even be rescued by one.

When they went around another turn in the trail, four people from the falls were coming toward them. In the lead was the dog. Natalia eyed it nervously. She didn't like the fact that it was off its leash. Dogs could bite or snap or otherwise be unpredictable. Its ears stood straight up, and its blue eyes were a striking contrast to its flat brown coat with a white splash on the chest.

Thirty feet behind the dog was the college-age couple it belonged to—the tall, skinny white guy in cutoffs, with the leash draped around his neck like a scarf, and the Hispanic girl in flip-flops, a blue-and-white beach towel draped over her bare shoulders. Behind them was an African American man with graying hair. He was holding the hand of a lighter-skinned boy who looked about eight.

Wyatt stepped into the middle of the path and raised his hands. "Hey, guys—I'm sorry, but we can't get out this way. There's a fire about a half mile back."

"What? A forest fire?" The older man wrapped one arm around the boy. He pulled him close, ignoring the kid's attempts to squirm away.

"Really?" The girl's eyes went wide.

"Blue!" Her boyfriend patted his thigh, and the dog came to his side. He snapped on the leash.

Wyatt pointed the way they had come. "We're not fire experts, but we figured we'd be safest by the water. If I climb up above the falls, I think I might be able to get cell service. Then I could ask 9-1-1 what to do."

This time there wasn't any argument or discussion, just a hurried push to get back to where they had started. When they reached Basin Falls, there were only three people left. The sweaty white guy was finishing up the last of his Gatorade. An older white woman wearing a tan sun hat and an old-fashioned pack was sitting on a boulder, watching the falls. And the dark-haired guy who had passed them on their way out was facing toward the trail, staring up at the sky. None of them were near each other.

"Hey! People! Listen up!" Wyatt waved his arms, but it was difficult to compete with the sight and sound of falling water.

Natalia slid off her backpack and found the gear she had bought at REI. She pulled out the cord holding a bright orange whistle and put it to her lips. Even over the rush of the waterfall, the sound was piercing. The other people's heads turned.

Wyatt put his hands around his mouth and shouted. "Hey, you guys, there's a fire blocking the trail." He pointed at the top of the falls. "I'm going to get up higher and see if I can get cell service."

He headed toward a faint line of trampled brush that led to the top of the falls. Natalia followed, her stomach twisting. At the bottom of the slope was a sign bolted to a tree. The top had the word "NO" in big white letters on a red background. In full, it read, "No cliff jumping or diving into Basin Falls. Three people have died trying. $500 fine."

"Do you really think it's safe to go up there?" she asked as he scrambled up on a boulder.

He looked over his shoulder. "Don't worry. I have no plans to try diving. Want to come up with me?"

"I'll just slow you down," Natalia said, which was true but not the truth. She was afraid of heights. "Just promise you'll be careful."

"Of course. But don't worry, I'll be fine." Wyatt started to clamber up the rocky hillside. Her heart in her mouth, Natalia watched him go.

# CHAPTER 4

# EXTREME DANGER

## 7:23 P.M.

AS NATALIA WATCHED, WYATT scrambled up the steep hill. He was in the full sun, but down here, in the shadows by the water, the light was changing as the sun got lower in the sky. Long, slanted rays revealed that smoke was beginning to reach them. How long until the fire did?

To calm herself, she took a deep breath, regretting it when she tasted the smoke. Around her, the other people were gradually coalescing, all of them looking up, focused on Wyatt.

Before joining them, the guy who had passed them on the way in tossed the bottle cap he'd been carrying into the water. Natalia didn't bother to hide her disgusted look. What a jerk! All those cargo pockets and he couldn't be bothered to pack out a single bottle cap? The bottle it belonged to had probably been tossed into the bushes along the way here. He met her glare with narrowed eyes.

Now he challenged her. "Are you *sure* there's a fire? I was just through there like a half hour ago and I didn't see any fire."

"Well, there's one now." She waved at the particles

floating in the sunbeams. "You can see the smoke in the air."

The girl in the flip-flops pointed at Wyatt. Her nails were painted purple. "So that's your boyfriend up there?"

"Um, we work together at an ice cream shop in Portland." Natalia gave the other girl a weak smile. "This was kind of our first date."

"Some first date!" She rolled her eyes. "My name's Beatriz."

"Natalia." She pointed up the hill. "And that's Wyatt."

With her thumb, Beatriz gestured back at the guy with the dog, who was standing a little apart from everyone. "My boyfriend, Marco. And the dog's named Blue." Knuckling the top of Blue's head, Marco nodded at them. He was skinny with a mop of streaked blond hair. His shorts, with hacked-off legs of different lengths, had clearly once been jeans.

Everyone else introduced themselves. The older guy was Darryl, and his grandson was named Zion. AJ was the stocky guy in boots that looked as new as Natalia's. Susan had an old-fashioned pack made of green canvas and gray curls peeking out from her sun hat. The jerk was the last one to give his name—Jason.

Wyatt was nearly at the top when suddenly his left foot slipped on some loose rocks. As Natalia gasped, he caught himself.

"He looks like he knows what he's doing, honey," Susan said.

Natalia wasn't reassured. This was real life. If Wyatt fell, he could be badly hurt. Maybe even killed. If he broke his back or even a leg, how much could she really do with her first aid kit? The Red Cross class she took every summer was predicated on what to do in the few minutes you might have to wait for an ambulance.

Wyatt finally reached the top. He turned and waved. Even though he was a good ten feet from the edge, Natalia wished he would take a few more steps back. After pulling out his phone, he extended his arm and turned in a circle, squinting. He slowed, moved the phone toward him, frowned, stopped. Then he seemed to have found a small sweet spot. He began tapping on the screen, still at arm's length.

Beatriz clapped. "He must have a signal!"

Gingerly, Wyatt tilted the phone so the speaker was closest to him. The rush of the falls made it impossible to hear anything he said. He listened with his head cocked, nodded a couple of times, and spoke very little. Finally, he turned in the direction of the parking lot, shading his eyes with his free hand. But when he tried to relay what he saw, it was clear from his frustrated expression and how he moved the phone that he had lost the signal.

After a few minutes of trying and failing to find it again, Wyatt pocketed the phone and started back. Before he was even halfway down, people were shouting questions.

"What did they say?" AJ yelled.

Darryl cupped his hands around his mouth. "When are they coming?"

Wyatt held up one hand to tell them to wait. Finally he reached the last big boulder. Rather than trying to climb down, he crouched and jumped, landing with bent knees.

"Okay, okay." He held up both hands as more questions flew. "Just let me talk. 9-1-1 patched me through to the sheriff's department. They already knew about the fire, but now they're alerting the Forest Service that we're here. They said we should wait for further instructions."

"*Wait?* Is that such a good idea?" AJ gestured at the increasingly murky air. "It's already getting smokier. What if the fire gets here before they do?"

"I took a look while I was up there," Wyatt said. "It's still maybe three-quarters of a mile away."

"Could you see that couple who kept going?" Natalia asked. It was hard to breathe when she thought of Trask's chubby hands clutched in his father's hair.

He shook his head. "But there's a lot of tree cover. And there are breaks in the fire. Maybe they found a way through."

"If that fire gets a wind behind it," Darryl said, "it'll eat up that three-quarters of a mile before you know it." His sunglasses made his expression unreadable, but his words made Zion press his face into his grandpa's round belly.

Wyatt's mouth twisted. "They said that one problem is that the best way out is already blocked by the Cougar Creek fire."

"How are we supposed to get instructions, anyway?" Beatriz asked. "None of us can get a signal down here, and you barely got one up there."

AJ pointed. "Look!"

Four helicopters appeared on the horizon. The three largest carried giant cloth buckets. One by one, they released their contents. Two were filled with what must have been fire retardant. It was the bright red of fresh blood. The third dropped what looked like water.

Three helicopters trying to put out the flames. Not the one Wyatt had thought might do the trick. But that was when they'd first spotted the fire. How far had it spread since? Would three be enough?

But maybe it didn't even matter, because the fourth helicopter, the smallest and the only one without a bucket, was buzzing closer.

With the rest, Natalia jumped and cheered, shouted and waved. She wasn't worried the pilot didn't see them. It was just a way of channeling her anxiety. Soon they would be safe.

The chopper hovered directly above them. Leaves and even small sticks began to rise in the air, swirling in the wind created by the turning blades.

Beatriz wrinkled her nose. "Do you think it can hold all of us?" She had to raise her voice to be heard over the rotors.

"If not, Zion should be on the first trip out." Darryl said. "And, Susan, maybe you, too."

"But it's getting dark," AJ said. "Can that thing even land at night? What if it can only take one trip?"

Instead of landing, the helicopter began to lift higher. As the group fell into stunned silence, it started to fly away.

"Maybe they're going back to get a bigger one," Beatriz said. "So there's room for all of us."

A shiver danced across Natalia's skin as she watched the helicopter grow smaller and smaller. She must have made some small sound of protest, because Wyatt whispered, "Are you okay?" in her ear.

She kept her voice low. "This was just supposed to be a day trip. I don't want to get stuck here overnight."

"I don't think we will be." Wyatt's tone was matter-of-fact. Natalia thought he was trying to reassure her, until he added, "The thing is, up there I could see pretty far. And all I could see was fire. I think it's too late for those helicopters to stop it. And that means we won't be able to stay put. I've got a map and compass in my pack. I'm going to figure out how we can get out of here."

*All I could see was fire.* Shock kept her from protesting.

Shrugging off his backpack, Wyatt rummaged through it until he found the map. He was tracing his finger over contour lines when Zion shouted and pointed. The small helicopter was coming back.

This time it dropped a weighted plastic bag. It landed on the other side of a small creek that fed the falls.

Barking, Blue ran toward it, with Marco splashing right behind. He picked up the bag and opened it. Inside was a rock and a piece of paper. While people shouted at him to read it, Natalia just watched his face. First his eyes narrowed, and then they went wide. He raised them from the note to the helicopter, which was again lifting up. Already flying away, without a single one of them on board.

"It says, 'Fire spreading.'" Marco stopped to cough, then cleared his throat. "'Extreme danger. Head to Sky Bridge.'"

# CHAPTER 5

# BLACKENED LACE

7:56 P.M.

*EXTREME DANGER.* **THEY WERE** trapped. How many dreams had Natalia had about that very situation? But those dreams were always about being confined in a house, flames blocking an exit. This wasn't a matter of finding another door or breaking out a window. If the fire kept rolling forward, consuming everything it its path, was there even a way out?

Her pulse a thrum in her throat, Natalia looked down the trail. The air was definitely thicker, but she didn't see any flames. Yet.

"Sky Bridge?" Susan's brows drew together, but then her expression cleared. "Really? That's where I was going."

"How far away is that?" AJ adjusted his pack, briefly exposing his hairy belly.

Wyatt looked up from his map. "A couple of miles."

But this was trail miles. Natalia guessed it would probably take an hour to get there.

"And then what?" Darryl's sunglasses reflected twin orange disks of the sun, low on the horizon. "There's a town? A road?"

"Sky Bridge is just a wooden footbridge over a slot

canyon," Wyatt said. "The trail splits on the other side. There's no roads or towns for a long ways. Just forest."

Marco put his arm around Beatriz. "Maybe they're going to have a ranger meet us there to lead us out."

"Hey," Darryl called out, looking up the trail. "Where are you going?"

Jason was already fifty feet away. He spoke over his shoulder. "I'm not going to keep sitting around here waiting for the fire to catch up with us."

"Does he mean we're going to get burned up?" Zion asked in a high voice.

"Of course not." Natalia joined the chorus responding with varying degrees of conviction. Just last week, she had read about a family who died when a fast-moving California wildfire trapped them in their own home. After wrapping themselves in wet blankets they had sheltered in the bathtub, but the fire hadn't cared. Natalia had had to use every trick Dr. Paris had taught her to stop obsessing about their last moments.

"Hang on, Jason," Wyatt said. "It will be safer if we stay together as a group."

"Listen to Mr. Boy Scout," Jason scoffed. But he stopped walking.

"Actually, I'm an Eagle Scout." Wyatt shrugged on his pack. He still held his map, now folded. "But Jason's right. We do need to leave. We should try to cover as much distance as possible while we still have daylight. And since there's a good chance we're going to still be hiking after it gets dark, everyone should try to preserve cell phone battery power for the flashlights."

Filled with nervous energy, the group fell into a long, straggling line, with Jason in the lead and Wyatt bringing up the rear. Despite what Wyatt had said, Natalia didn't think they were really a group at all. They were just nine people with nothing in common except bad luck. Most of them weren't even prepared for a longer hike.

Jason only had on tennis shoes and wasn't carrying a pack. Behind Jason were Marco and Beatriz. Marco had unclipped Blue's leash and draped it around his neck, but the dog stayed close, his nose occasionally bumping the back of Marco's knees. Marco wore Tevas and a small day pack, while Beatriz carried only a water bottle and the striped beach towel. Her heels kept sliding out of her flip-flops. Marco had one hand under her elbow, trying to steady her. His other hand now held a blue inhaler, which he took a puff from.

Next was Susan. Judging by her old-fashioned pack, she had plenty of hiking experience, but she was also well past retirement age. Still, aided by trekking poles, she was moving steadily.

Behind Susan was Zion. He was towing Darryl by the hand, commenting on every rock and root. Neither one of them was wearing a pack.

AJ was right in front of Natalia, close enough she could hear his labored breathing. But he had a good-sized pack on his back.

They'd gone only a couple of hundred yards up the trail when a shout came from behind them. It was a woman's voice. "Wait! Stop! Help us!"

A bolt of adrenaline ran up Natalia's spine. Already

knowing it had to be bad, she turned. It was the couple with the toddler, the ones who had insisted on seeing the fire for themselves. But now the child carrier holding Trask was on his mom's slight back, bending her nearly double. The toddler's face was wet with tears, sweat, and snot.

Stumbling in their wake was the husband. Half his light blue shirt was gone. The remaining edges looked like blackened lace. The exposed skin of his upper left arm and chest was shiny and red.

He had been burned.

## CHAPTER 6

# WHAT IF IT WAS YOU?

### 8:08 P.M.

**AT THE SIGHT OF** his burns, Natalia's vision went blurry. Blood roared in her ears.

"Oh my God." Susan put her hand to her chest. "What happened?"

"What do you think happened?" Jason snorted as Darryl tried to turn Zion's face away. "Dude got burned."

"You were right," the dad said to Wyatt. "We couldn't get through. I got too close, looking for a way out. A spark landed on my T-shirt. I tried to beat it out." He raised his right hand. The palm was bright red, dotted with yellow.

Natalia didn't have to imagine his agony. She knew. And she also knew she should be helping him, but she couldn't seem to move. Her head filled with static.

"Okay." Wyatt sucked in a breath. "Are you the only one who was hurt?" He looked at the wife and Trask.

"Just me, thank God." The burned man sat down heavily on a boulder.

"I have some first aid training," Wyatt said. "Can I help you?"

When the other man nodded, Wyatt said in an artificially calm voice, "My name's Wyatt. What's your name? I already know your little guy is named Trask." As he spoke, he pulled a battered first aid kit from his backpack and pulled on a pair of blue gloves.

"Ryan. And my wife is Lisa."

"First we have to cool the burns down," Wyatt said. "I'm going to need a clean cloth, like a T-shirt or bandanna, and some clean water."

"On it," Marco said.

Lisa was standing with her hands braced on her knees, panting from the combined weight of her kid and her worry.

Natalia forced herself to move. Not away from the burned man, but toward him. The Red Cross training, practiced year after year, began to kick in.

She leaned down and murmured to Wyatt, "Do you need help? I'm Red Cross certified." Could he hear the quaver in her voice?

He exhaled in relief. "Yeah, I'd love it. It's ABC, right?"

She nodded. ABC was one of a half-dozen mnemonics to help remember what to do and in what order. *A* was *airway*. A mouth full of chew, gum, or vomit would mess things up if they had to start CPR.

As she got out her own first aid kit and found her gloves, Wyatt asked, "Okay, Ryan, can you open your mouth? Do you have anything in it?"

Ryan shook his head as he obediently parted his lips. The inside of his mouth looked pink and healthy. No signs of soot. His face wasn't burned. His hair didn't look singed, although it was hard to tell for sure because it was black to begin with. But this close, they would probably smell the horrible stench if it had been.

"Great." Somehow, Wyatt managed to sound almost cheerful, but Natalia reminded herself that the calmer they were, or at least pretended to be, the calmer Ryan would be. She could not afford to pay attention to the memories crowding back.

Off to the side, AJ was helping Lisa remove the child carrier that held Trask. It had a kickstand, so when they put it on the ground he ended up suspended, his little legs dangling a few inches above the ground. His crying had been reduced to an occasional sob.

She couldn't afford to think about the toddler, either.

Marco reappeared with a folded blue bandanna and an unopened bottle of drinking water.

"Thank you," Natalia said. After wetting the bandanna, she put it on the worst part of Ryan's shoulder. He sucked air through his teeth. Under the cool, wet cloth, his skin still radiated heat.

"Can you hold this in place for me with your burned hand?" she asked. He gingerly rested his hand on top.

If burns covered 15 or 20 percent of the body, it could be fatal. The flat of a hand, including the fingers, was equal to 1 percent. She measured with her eyes. Her shoulders loosened. Ryan's burns only covered 3 or 4 percent.

"*B* is *breathing*, right?" Wyatt looked at Natalia for confirmation. She nodded.

He turned back to Ryan. "Can you take two deep breaths for me?"

When he did, they didn't sound labored, and he didn't cough.

"Awesome," Wyatt said.

Still, Natalia thought, what if Ryan *had* breathed in a lot of smoke? It might have inflamed his lungs and airway. If they started swelling, even CPR wouldn't save him. Her own breathing sped up. She reminded herself that Ryan had been in the outdoors. Not trapped in a house where the smoke was filled with toxic fumes from burning drywall, synthetic carpeting, and household chemicals. Where there was no place for it to go except in your lungs.

"And *C* is . . . *cardiac*?" Wyatt ventured.

She forced herself to focus. "Close. Circulation. But it's pretty easy to see he's not bleeding. Let me just check his pulse." She took Ryan's left wrist, rolling her gloved fingertips until she found the notch. Fast but not shallow. She knew she should count the beats, but her thoughts were still skittering. "Great," she said, not elaborating, as she released his wrist.

"How long is this going to take?" Jason demanded from behind them.

"Just shut up and let her help him," Beatriz said. "What if it was you?"

"Okay, let's see what we're dealing with." Wyatt plucked the wet cloth from Ryan's shoulder. Part of the burn was obscured by Ryan's T-shirt.

From her first aid kit, Natalia took out the small pair of shears with slanted blades. But looking closer at his shoulder, she hesitated. The remaining fabric seemed fused to his skin.

Ryan twisted his head and grimaced. "I think it melted. Hundred percent polyester. Great for hiking. Not so great, it turns out, for forest fires." When she leaned closer and squinted at an odd black spot on his biceps, he added, "And that's just a Swoosh tattoo. I work at Nike."

"Let's leave his shirt be." Wyatt looked at Natalia. "How many burn pads do we have?"

She started with her own first aid kit. The contents were all neatly organized and labeled. But there was only one burn pad, just three by four inches. That wasn't nearly enough.

Wyatt's kit had clearly seen heavy use, with different brands of supplies and some half-used tubes of ointment. There was even a flattened roll of silver duct tape, the cardboard center removed.

But just one more burn pad. Which meant they had enough for Ryan's shoulder, but not his hand. Or his hand, and only half his shoulder. She and Wyatt exchanged a glance.

"Those are second-degree burns, right?" Marco leaned in, his expression curious. "Because there's blisters."

"They're called partial-thickness burns now," she said. "But it's same thing."

"All I know is they hurt like hell," Ryan said through clenched teeth.

Better they hurt than they didn't. That was what the nurses had told her. Natalia didn't think Ryan would find it any more comforting than she had.

Forcing herself to take a deep breath, she mentally repeated the Red Cross instructor's advice. "Do the best you can with what you have." It was similar to Dr. Paris's advice: "Control what you can and leave the rest."

"Let's use one pad on his shoulder and the other on his right hand," she said to Wyatt. "It's his dominant hand, which means he's still going to use it even if he doesn't mean to."

She peeled open the packaging. In her head, the Red Cross instructor said, "Anything that opens like string cheese—that you grab at the top and pull down on each side—is sterile." And sterile was important, because Ryan's burn was basically an open wound.

Careful not to touch the pad, she laid it gently on top of the worst part of the burn.

"Ow!" He jerked.

She winced. "Sorry." In the smoky light and with Ryan's naturally darker skin, it was hard to tell how he was doing. Did he look pale? Was his skin clammy? She wasn't sure. Maybe. But even if Ryan was starting to go into shock, they couldn't exactly have him lie down while they elevated his feet and waited for help. Even though she felt helpless, she was glad her thinking was no longer as muddled.

Natalia lightly pressed the pad into place, glad to see the skin around it turn paler as she did. Skin that didn't blanch—that stayed red under pressure—would mean the burns were worse than they looked. Half her supply of antibiotic ointment went to smearing one side of a piece of dry gauze, which she put on a different section of his shoulder. She wrapped both with more gauze. Then she applied the second burn pad to his blistered palm and wrapped it with the last of the gauze from her kit, ignoring how the breath hissed between his teeth.

Now that she actually was using the first aid kit, it felt more like a toy. She poked through the remaining supplies. There weren't many more bandages, and a bunch of stuff just seemed useless. A triangular bandage. Four large safety pins. Two cotton swabs. Six antiseptic wipes. A bunch of Band-Aids. Short metal tweezers in a tiny plastic vial. A pencil and paper to record notes. Wyatt had a few more things but not many. If anyone else got seriously hurt, what would they do?

She also had little packages of medications that Wyatt didn't: ibuprofen, acetaminophen, aspirin, antihistamine, and antidiarrheal pills. The acetaminophen wouldn't do anything for swelling. And if there was any bleeding she'd missed, the aspirin would only make it worse. Opening up a package, she shook two pills into Ryan's good left hand. "Here's some ibuprofen."

"Don't you have anything stronger?" He shaped his mouth into something like a smile. "Like whiskey?"

"Whiskey wouldn't keep the swelling down, and those will." She handed him the half-empty bottle of water. "Keep drinking this. Little sips."

Before they started off again, Wyatt moved to Ryan's wife. "Hey, Lisa." His voice was soft. "Why don't you let me take Trask? I'll give my pack to someone else."

"No." She took a step back, shaking her head. "I can carry him."

"I'm sure you can, but we're going to need to move

fast. And if I carry Trask, it'll be easier for you to keep an eye on how Ryan's doing."

"Let him do it, Lisa," Ryan said.

There was a general shuffling of belongings. Marco gave his small pack to Beatriz and then took Wyatt's. With assistance from Lisa and Natalia, Wyatt hoisted Trask onto his back. The toddler only fussed a little.

"Damn it!" Beatriz said.

"What?"

Her hands were on her hips. "That stupid Jason guy must have taken off again."

And while a few people complained or cursed, no one was really surprised.

# CHAPTER 7

# ORANGE TWILIGHT
8:28 P.M.

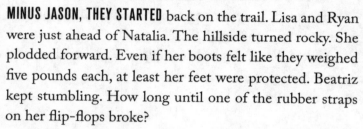

**MINUS JASON, THEY STARTED** back on the trail. Lisa and Ryan were just ahead of Natalia. The hillside turned rocky. She plodded forward. Even if her boots felt like they weighed five pounds each, at least her feet were protected. Beatriz kept stumbling. How long until one of the rubber straps on her flip-flops broke?

Wyatt was still bringing up the rear, if you didn't count Trask. When Natalia looked back, the toddler was fast asleep, his head tipped forward to rest on Wyatt's shoulder. She turned back around, glad Trask was out of her direct line of sight. He reminded her too much of Conner.

She desperately wished she were anyplace but on this trail. Home. At the Dairy Barn. Or back in Wyatt's Toyota with her feet bare and the windows rolled down, the wind tugging at her hair as the tires hummed underneath them.

Earlier the sky had been bright blue, seemingly limitless. But now the gathering darkness combined with the smoke to create an eerie orange twilight haze. When Natalia licked her lips, she tasted ash.

Her shirt was sticking to her back, and sweat trickled

down her spine. She eyed Ryan. He was actually managing to keep a steady pace. If he was in shock, it must be mild.

Ahead of Ryan, Darryl slipped a granola bar from his pocket into Zion's palm. He bent down to whisper in his ear. He was still wearing sunglasses, even though the sun was starting to set behind them. As furtively as a kid could, Zion unwrapped the bar and began to sneak bits into his mouth.

"I'm so glad you were there to remind me what to do," Wyatt said. "I mean, I know some first aid because of Scouts, but it feels like you know a lot more."

"I take classes at the Red Cross." The idea had originally been Dr. Paris's, a way to help Natalia feel more in control. She retook them every summer to keep her certification current. "I want to be a doctor." Doctors saved lives. That wouldn't make up for her failure. Nothing would. But the idea allowed her to keep living. After pushing a branch away from her face, she continued to hold it for Wyatt.

When he placed his hand on the branch, his fingers brushed hers. "Plus you have a much better first aid kit than I do. Like you had shears and all those little packets of medications. Mine's pretty basic."

Natalia had been thinking about her kit. "I don't know how much help it will be if something else goes wrong. On the front it says it has more than a hundred pieces, but there's a lot of filler. It's got five or six knuckle bandages, for example, and how often do you really need even one? And that was my only pair of gloves."

"In some ways, I don't think it really matters what's in

your kit. What matters more is what you do with it. And I think most girls would have just been freaking out."

Natalia felt a flush of pride—and also the need to set him straight. "That's not just a girl thing. It looked to me like most people were freaked out when they saw those burns."

"Fair point."

"Sorry I froze at the beginning." She sidestepped a gnarled root. "But I've had some personal experience with burns." The words slipped past her lips before she had time to think.

Wyatt weighed this information, then asked, "Is that why you're afraid of fire?"

"Yeah." Why had she brought it up? It was the worst thing that had ever happened to her. "But I shouldn't have mentioned it. I don't want to think about or talk about it right now. I just want to get out of here. I wish we could fly instead of walking." After taking a particularly long step to avoid a divot in the trail, she changed the subject. "Why do you care so much about keeping us together? Jason's a jerk. Who cares if he went off by himself?"

"If we stick together, then we're stronger. Everyone has something different to contribute. That's why I like scouting. I like being part of a group."

As if to underscore the point, ahead of them AJ offered his hand to Susan as she clambered over a rocky part of the trail.

"You're not just part of this group," Natalia pointed out. "You're pretty much leading it. Even the adults are listening to you."

"Somebody had to take charge. When you put a group under stress, it either pulls together or falls apart. I'm trying to make sure we pull together."

Her nose was running, partly from smoke and partly from exertion. She took a tissue from her pants pocket.

"Since we could be stuck out here for a while," Wyatt said, "you might want to use your sleeve for your nose and save that for later."

"But why—" Natalia figured it out and shut up. She was definitely *not* going to pee—or, worse yet, poop—in the woods. Still, she followed his suggestion, even though it felt gross to smear her nose on her sleeve. After she did, she sniffed. "It doesn't smell quite as smoky now."

"I think your nose just gets used to it. It's like when you're in a freshly painted room and after a while you stop smelling it. Humans—all animals, really—are hardwired to notice contrasts, not constants."

"Like how they say not to run if you meet a cougar, because it will want to chase you?" She had tried to prepare for this hike by reading a bunch of worst-case scenarios.

"Yeah. It's why animals like rabbits are so good at staying still. Because staying still is sometimes the best thing to do."

While Wyatt was talking, Susan let AJ go on ahead. She stood and waited for them with an anxious expression.

"How are you doing, Susan?" Wyatt asked. "Are you holding up okay?"

"I know I should remember, honey, but where are we going again?" She bit her lip.

"Sky Bridge," he answered.

The older woman snapped her fingers. "Right. That's where I was going. I love that bridge." She looked from Wyatt to Natalia. "Are either of you wearing a hand clock?"

They exchanged a puzzled look, before understanding dawned. Susan must mean a watch. Her phrasing made her sound like someone who spoke English as a second language, only she didn't have an accent.

Natalia slipped the corner of her phone out of her pocket. "Eight thirty-nine."

The older woman nodded. "So sunset's not far away."

"Yeah, it will be after sunset by the time we get to the bridge." Wyatt pressed his lips together. "Maybe that's actually better." He and Susan exchanged a look.

"Why would that be better?" Natalia asked.

"The slot canyon it goes over is pretty deep," Wyatt said. "That's why it's called Sky Bridge."

Great. Natalia didn't like heights. Or enclosed spaces. Or swimming if she couldn't touch the bottom and keep her head out of water.

Or, of course, fire.

"Why is it called a slot canyon?" she asked, trying to distract herself as they all kept moving closer to it.

"It's what happens when you pit water against rock. First there's just a tiny crack with water flowing through it. But over thousands of years that stream of water carves a narrow canyon that just gets deeper and deeper."

"Huh," she said, trying to act as if the thought weren't completely terrifying.

Thirty minutes later, they rounded a bend and there it was. Sky Bridge. Even though the sun had slipped below the horizon, it was still light enough to see it. Made of wood, it was just wide enough for one person. The drop to the water far below had to be at least seventy-five feet.

But that wasn't why the group was starting to freak out.

And it wasn't from the sight of Jason, still on the same side of the slot canyon as them.

It was the fact that there was a tall makeshift gate across the bridge.

And it was padlocked.

## CHAPTER 8

# DISCO BOOTS
9:12 P.M.

MARCO TURNED ON THE flashlight on his phone, illuminating the paper sign duct-taped to the middle of the gate.

*Trail closed due to fire.*

"Why did the helicopter pilot tell us to come here when the stupid bridge is blocked?" Jason gave the gate a shake. "He trapped us." No one had confronted him—or greeted him, either.

Adrenaline zapped through Natalia. Behind them the sky glowed orange, and it wasn't just from the remains of the sunset.

"They probably have no idea this gate's even here," Wyatt said. "I'll bet in the last couple of days some ranger threw this up to keep people from taking the Cougar Creek trail on the other side. They didn't realize there was going to be another fire. And now the first responders must be scrambling, trying to figure out who all's in the woods and where to tell them to go."

The gate did look improvised. They must have been limited by what they could carry up here. It was really just two pieces of chain-link fence, each about six feet high by five feet wide, overlapped and then chained together in the middle. The fencing had been anchored to the narrow bridge by more chains threaded through the handrails. The ends of the makeshift gate stuck out on either side of the footbridge.

Taking baby steps, Natalia got close enough that she could look down to the bottom of the narrow canyon. The others crowded around. It was a straight drop, far deeper than it was wide.

And then suddenly someone shoved her hard from behind. She shrieked as she fought to keep her balance. Pebbles skittered out from under her boot like marbles, then disappeared over the edge. Leaning back desperately, she pinwheeled her arms.

And then hands grabbed her.

"Careful!" Jason shouted, dragging her back.

"Whoa there!" Darryl said.

"Are you okay?" Wyatt's face was drawn with concern.

Before she answered, she put about twenty feet between her and the edge. "Someone pushed me!"

Her heart was a bird trapped in the cage of her ribs. Her gaze jumped from face to face. No one looked guilty, just puzzled.

"Why would anyone do that?" Marco asked.

"I didn't see anything," AJ said.

Already Natalia's certainty was evaporating. Someone had definitely pressed her hard. Not just a press, but a shove. But maybe it had been an accident, a person losing their own balance who now didn't want to admit having accidentally touched her. After all, why would anyone want to hurt her?

She decided to let it go. "I felt this pressure on my lower back. Maybe I overreacted to someone touching me. I was already anxious being so close to the edge. I just wanted to see if there was another way across."

Seemingly unfazed by the drop, Jason leaned over. "Maybe we could climb down, cross over, and then climb back up the other side."

"And how would we do that?" Ryan didn't bother to hide his sarcasm. Ferns and moss had managed to find footholds in the steep rock, but there was no way a person could. "We don't have rope or carabiners or climbing harnesses or basically anything. And even if we did, that's freaking white water down there." He held up his bandaged hand. "Half of us would never be able to get down, let alone up."

Beatriz tilted her head back. "Could we climb over the gate?"

"Same problem, B," Marco said. "Some people would have a real hard time getting over." He gave the gate a shake. "And it seems kind of wobbly. If anyone fell off while they were climbing over and missed landing on the bridge . . ."

Wyatt raised his hands, linked his fingers on the chain links, and then gave the gate a hard shove. It groaned in protest.

The sound woke Trask, who had been asleep on Wyatt's back. He started crying and kicking. "Mama! Mama!"

Both parents hurried up. "I'm right here, honey," Lisa said. Ryan patted Trask's back with his unburned hand.

The sight of the little boy rubbing his fists against his eyes made Natalia feel like she was fracturing. For the past six years, she had avoided toddlers the way she avoided fires. And now here she was with both.

"Can you set him down?" Lisa asked Wyatt. "He's not going to stop crying unless I can hold him."

Wyatt unbuckled the waistband of the child carrier, and Lisa helped him maneuver it off, Ryan awkwardly trying to help with his good hand. After unbuckling the child safety strap, Lisa lifted him out and held him on her hip, pressing his face to her chest. Trask was wearing baby overalls, the kind that unsnapped at the legs for diaper changes.

Wyatt started examining the chains and locks, pushing and pulling on various pieces. Everyone else took a break, setting down heavy packs, taking sips of water, or surreptitiously nibbling on trail mix. The air was thick with ash. Still coughing, Marco pulled the inhaler from his pocket, shook it, and took another puff.

"Where are we?" Susan scanned the group, looking confused.

"We're at Sky Bridge, Susan," Natalia said.

The older woman started. "Who are you?"

"I'm . . . I'm Natalia." Maybe it was just hard for her to make out people's faces in the dim and smoky light.

Susan wiped a hand over her face. "Oh, right, honey. Sky Bridge."

Beatriz limped up to them. "Hey, Natalia, Do you have a Band-Aid I could have?"

Natalia looked down and winced. The sides of Beatriz's

heels were bruised and oozing blood. "It looks like you need more than that."

"It's my own fault for wearing stupid flip-flops instead of real shoes. We've been to the falls a bunch. But I never thought of it as, like, you know, the actual wilderness."

Even if Natalia used up every Band-Aid she had, including the knuckle ones, they wouldn't do much to protect Beatriz's feet against further damage.

Ryan spoke up. "With your flip-flops, you've actually got the sole of a shoe. You just don't have the vamp and the quarter—the top parts. But there might be a way to fix that." He looked around. "Does anyone have an extra pair of socks Beatriz could use?"

"I do," Wyatt said, surprising no one. After leaving the gate and locating his pack, he pulled out a pair of gray wool socks and handed them to Beatriz. "These might be a little big for you."

"Big is good," Ryan said. "I'm thinking if we pull them over Beatriz's flip-flops they'll stop sliding around. Kind of like a slipper sock, only inside out."

Wyatt nodded. "You work on that and I'll work on how to get us across." He returned to the puzzle of the gate.

"Mind being my hands, Natalia?" Ryan asked.

"Not at all."

The three of them sat down. Natalia pulled Beatriz's right foot onto her lap and started using Band-Aids on the worst cuts.

Wyatt began pushing at the top of the makeshift gate.

Marco joined in on the other side. "On my count," Wyatt said. "One, two, three, push!"

They grunted, the chains squealed, and when they stopped thirty seconds later, it looked like they had managed to move it an inch or two.

Wyatt's voice cracked with excitement. "I think if we keep pushing the top, we could pivot it from vertical to horizontal. Then we could crawl underneath."

Darryl, AJ, and Jason joined them. Susan made no move to get up. She was sitting on a boulder, shoulders drooping, her face slack and vacant. Zion squeezed in next to his grandpa, but he was too short to reach as high as the others.

"Hey, buddy, why don't you pull at the bottom?" Wyatt suggested to Zion. He counted again. "Okay, one, two, three!"

After covering up the worst of Beatriz's cuts, Natalia tugged a sock over one flip-flop, working to get the sock's heel to match the sandal's heel. The other girl sucked in her breath but didn't complain. Blue nosed her with a low whine. Beatriz put her arm around him and gave him a squeeze.

"He seems pretty chill," Natalia observed as Susan reached out to pet him. Dogs usually made her nervous, but she was starting to relax around Blue.

"He's the best. My sister's kids like to dress him up, and he just sits there and lets them. Even when we all laugh at how ridiculous he looks."

Natalia finished tugging on the second sock. As the

guys worked on the gate, Beatriz got to her feet. She took a couple of tentative steps and then some more confident ones. "That feels good. Way more like a real shoe. Thanks, Ryan."

"Slipper socks have the sole on the outside. I'm worried the socks will wear out too fast." He snapped the fingers of his unburned hand. "Didn't I see some duct tape in Wyatt's first aid kit?"

When Natalia asked if they could use the duct tape, Wyatt nodded absently, focused on the progress they were making. She located it in his pack and held out the flattened roll to Ryan. "Do you think there's enough?"

He narrowed his eyes. "It's hard to say. Wrap the toes and heels first and then if there's enough you can fill in the rest."

Natalia tore off a strip. When she pressed it on she realized she hadn't made it long enough to meet at the top.

"For the next strip, try unwinding some tape and using the back to measure before you tear," Beatriz suggested.

Natalia did. Adding first a strip to the right foot and then to the left, she gradually wrapped up Beatriz's feet. Meanwhile, the bottom edge of the gate had now been forced about six inches above the ground. It wasn't yet big enough for even Zion to fit underneath, but they were definitely making progress. Everyone was panting from the pushing, so Wyatt called for a five-minute break.

After Natalia pressed the last piece of duct tape into place, Beatriz crowed, "Disco boots!" She leaned back and kicked her feet in the air.

"Just be careful," Ryan said. "They're probably slick."

Beatriz squeezed his good hand in thanks and then hugged Natalia. One of Beatriz's braids pressed into her cheek, and Natalia could smell the sweet, flowery scent of her shampoo.

As she looked over Beatriz's shoulder, her gaze snagged on AJ.

Even in the fading light, he looked pale and sweaty. He seemed to be panting. And he had one hand pressed to his chest.

"Are you okay, AJ?"

"It's just—my chest hurts." His panicked eyes met Natalia's. "I think I'm having a heart attack."

## CHAPTER 9

# FIVE THINGS YOU CAN SEE

9:28 P.M.

IGNORING HER OWN RACING heart, Natalia moved closer to AJ. "What makes you think you're having a heart attack?"

Any confidence she had gained evaporated. When it came to heart attacks, the Red Cross focused on the brief window between calling 9-1-1 and having real professionals take over.

But there were no paramedics out here. No ambulance. No sterile surfaces. No technology. No operating room. No board-certified surgeon. There was just Natalia and whatever she remembered from a few classes.

AJ's face was pale, his eyes wide. One hand was pressed against the center of his rib cage. "Every time I pushed on the gate, I felt this sharp pain in my chest. And now my heart is racing! What if it keeps going faster and faster?"

His expression made it clear he was sure of the answer: if it did, then he would die.

Wyatt whispered into Natalia's ear. "I know CPR, but not what to do with someone who has a pulse and is breathing."

"I'll try to figure out what's happening." She just

hoped it didn't come to needing Wyatt's skills. "Can you get people to give us some space?"

Wyatt clapped his hands. "Hey, guys, why don't we go back to pushing and let Natalia help AJ?" Beatriz took AJ's place at the gate. Even Lisa carefully set a half-asleep Trask on Ryan's lap, then joined the others. Only Susan stayed where she was.

It was a relief for Natalia not to have every eye on her. But if AJ really was having a heart attack, what could she realistically do?

Natalia could think of only one thing that might help. Digging through her first aid kit, she found the foil package of aspirin. "Do you have any problems with blood clotting?"

"No." AJ's voice shook, as if she was about to reveal some awful new piece of information. "Why?"

She pressed one of the two tablets into his sweaty hand. "Take this. But don't swallow it—chew it. It will get in your system faster." If it was a heart attack, aspirin would help inhibit the platelets that triggered clotting. Clots choked off blood flow, which led to tissue damage. An aspirin might lessen the effects.

And if AJ *wasn't* having a heart attack, one aspirin shouldn't hurt him.

She was getting ahead of herself. Natalia made herself go step by step. It took all her powers of concentration to ignore the smoke thickening the air and the roar of the fire as it ate its way toward them.

*ABC*. The only thing AJ had in his mouth was the aspirin he was chewing. When she asked him to take two deep breaths, they didn't sound labored. With a heart attack, deep breathing should hurt. But AJ didn't wince, his brows didn't draw together, his jaw wasn't clenched. She had to check his pulse, and this time it was important that she actually count. She called out to the others. "Does anyone have a watch with a second hand?"

"I have a Fitbit with a timer," Darryl said. He stepped away from the gate, with Zion trailing after him. He pushed his sunglasses to the top of his head as he raised his wrist.

"Dude, why are you even still wearing those things?" Jason asked. "If you haven't noticed, the sun's gone down."

It still wasn't fully dark, partly because it was summer. And partly because of the fire lighting the horizon. But it was pretty dim.

Darryl pressed his lips together. "They're prescription. My other glasses are back in the car. And without glasses, I can't see more than a couple of feet away."

"Come on, guys," Beatriz said. "We need to keep pushing." Next to her, Marco kept up a steady, light cough.

Natalia took AJ's wrist and rolled her fingers until she found the notch. "Okay, Darryl, tell me when to start and then time thirty seconds."

A light flared on Darryl's wrist. "Ready?" he said. "Go."

She started counting beats to herself, ignoring Wyatt's cries of, "One, two, three—push!" Under her fingertips, AJ's pulse was fast but steady. She had reached sixty-seven when Darryl said, "Stop."

"Thanks, Darryl," she said. "That's all I need."

As he and Zion rejoined the others, AJ asked, "So what's the number?"

"Your heart rate's 134."

"That's bad, isn't it?" The corners of his mouth pulled down.

It *was* high, especially since he was no longer exerting himself, but Natalia didn't think it was dangerously so. "It's actually not that bad. And it's strong and steady. Can you lift your T-shirt and show me exactly where it hurts?"

Tugging up the hem, AJ exposed a thatch of black hair. "Right here." He pressed his fingers in the center and then dropped his hand. Natalia pressed on the same spot, trying not to grimace at the feeling of matted, sweaty hair. He winced, sucking in air. "Yeah, that's it." His eyes shone wetly in the pulsing radiance cast by the fire.

Another mnemonic the Red Cross taught was SAMPLE: *Symptoms*, *Allergies*, *Medications*, *Pertinent medical history*, *Last ins and outs*, and *Events*.

"And how would you describe the pain?" Natalia buried the worrisome word in the middle of her list. "Throbbing, sharp, pressing, electric . . ."

"Sharp."

But people having heart attacks usually complained of pressure, not pain. They'd say it felt like having an elephant sit on their chest.

On the other hand, heart attacks were often brought on by exertion. And AJ had just been shoving on the gate as hard as he could. Natalia's thoughts spun tighter. What if he passed out?

"Do you have any other symptoms besides pain?"

"I just feel really bad. Like I'm going to die." His voice cracked.

At the gate, Wyatt called again, "One, two, three—push!" The wooden railings of the bridge groaned as the gate was pressed against them.

"Are you allergic to anything?"

A distracted shake of his head.

"Do you take any drugs, including, um"—she hesitated—"recreational?"

"Just Wellbutrin," he said softly. "For depression."

She pitched her voice for his ears alone. "I'm on Paxil." The thing was, Natalia was beginning to think they might have more in common than antidepressants. Because she had felt like AJ before. Like she was going to die. Not like she *wanted* to die, although she'd also experienced that. But like she was going to physically die right that very second.

"Have you recently seen a doctor for anything?"

"I had a physical a few months ago. The doctor said I was fine. Just overweight and out of shape. Which isn't fine at all. That's why I decided to start hiking." He made a sound like a laugh. "For my health."

"Believe it or not, this was supposed to be my introduction to the joy of hiking." Natalia smiled at AJ but got nothing back. She returned to her questions. "Have you had anything to eat or drink today?"

"Gatorade, chips, and a sandwich."

She lowered her voice. "And have you been peeing and pooping normally?"

"Yeah." AJ said it as if he was about to break. He had eyes for only the fire. The reddish light on his face flared and ebbed as the flames crept ever closer. His panic was catching.

What if they couldn't force the gate open before the fire caught up with them? What if AJ really was dying? Terrible what-ifs flooded in, just as a half hour earlier she had really believed that someone had pushed her. AJ's reaction felt all too familiar. But, Natalia realized, that familiarity meant she had some ideas about how to fix things. For both of them.

"Okay, AJ, I need you to do something for me." She was speaking, but it was Dr. Paris's words coming from her mouth. "I need you to tell me five things you can see, four things you can touch, three things you can hear, two things you can smell, and one thing you can taste."

He didn't respond.

"Five things you can see," she prompted.

AJ shook his head, swallowed, and then his gaze finally unlatched from the horizon. "Um, your face, that tree, the baby, the dog, and uh, your pack."

"Good! Now four things you can touch."

He focused on the ground around them. "That big rock, that plant with the white flowers, my boots, and um, I guess the ground." AJ set his palms on it, and she did as well. The cool dirt gave slightly under her hands.

"Okay, how about three things you can hear?"

"I can hear Wyatt counting. The water under the bridge." He paused and shivered. "And, um, sorry, the fire."

"It's okay. That's reality." Dr. Paris had taught Natalia how to walk that fine line of truth, to acknowledge what had happened, while not falling into fear or despair or self-hatred. It was a narrow path, but it still led out of the darkness. "And two things you can smell?"

"Smoke." He sniffed deeply, then a small smile raised his lips. "And me. For which I apologize."

She returned his smile. "I'm pretty sure we all smell bad. Now what's one thing you can taste?"

"My mouth tastes sour."

AJ's breathing had slowed, and fear no longer shadowed his face.

"How do you feel?" Natalia asked.

As he paused to think about it, the people pushing the gate let out a ragged cheer. Now it was nearly parallel with the bridge.

"Better. So what do you think's wrong with me?"

"I think it might actually have been a panic attack." Natalia chose the past tense on purpose. She wanted him to think of it as over. "I've had them before, too."

"You mean it's all in my head?"

She shaped Dr. Paris's words to her own use. "It's not like you were making it up. We all react to stressful events differently. There's no right or wrong way. The only wrong thing right now is the fire. You're having a normal reaction to an abnormal event." Getting to her feet, she offered him her hand. "We are ahead of the fire, and we are going to stay ahead of it. We will get out of this. We just have to keep moving and keep breathing."

"AJ's going to be okay," she announced to the group, hoping she was right.

While she was speaking, Jason was dropping to his hands and knees. He was the first to scuttle under the two-foot-high gap. Once past the gate, he got to his feet and walked the rest of the way across.

As the others began to crawl one by one under the tipped-sideways gate, Wyatt came back to Natalia. "Is AJ really okay?"

"I think so," she said. "The pain got better when I had him focus on other things. I think it was a panic attack. But even if I'm wrong, it doesn't change anything. We still need to get out of here."

As Wyatt nodded in agreement, Lisa came up to them. "I don't think there's enough room for you to crawl under there with Trask on your back. Maybe if we take him out of the carrier, I can get him to crawl ahead of me and I'll hold on to his foot."

They all looked at the bridge. Except for the handrails at the top and a single lengthwise board about knee-high, the sides of the bridge were open between the supports.

Marco took Blue's leash from around his neck and held it out. "What if you clipped the end onto the back of his overalls and then looped it around your wrist?"

"Thanks." Lisa took it. "That would work."

Because Wyatt wasn't needed to help with Trask now, he hung back to help the others get through. Pushing her pack ahead of her, Natalia went first. She wormed on her belly until she got past the gate. Then she got to her feet and put on her pack to walk the rest of the way. Even once she was on solid ground, she still felt tenuous.

Lisa nudged Trask ahead of her and then got to her feet and gathered him in her arms. Once she was on the other side of the bridge, she came up to Natalia.

"Do you mind holding him while I help my husband get under?"

"Sure," she said, holding out her arms before she could think better of it. Lisa handed him over and then unsnapped the dog leash.

Trask was warm and slightly sticky, too tired to even go stiff in her arms. He smelled a little bit sweet and a little bit sour, a mix of baby shampoo and urine from what had to be a soaked diaper. When he started to fuss, she automatically jigged up and down, rocking him lightly on her hip, ignoring the slightly squishy feeling of it. He slumped against her.

Memories came flooding back.

## CHAPTER 10

# WHAT CAN HAPPEN IN TEN MINUTES?

SIX YEARS EARLIER

**NATALIA LIFTED CONNER FROM** the car seat and set him on her hip while her mom unloaded the groceries. Conner slumped against her, warm and heavy and more than half-asleep. With her free hand, she pulled his green plaid blankie from the car, shook out the Goldfish crumbs, and tucked it between him and her side. Heaven help them all if it ever got lost.

Her brother was two, nine years younger than she was. Natalia's parents sometimes called him their miracle baby. Maybe they didn't realize how that sounded. Like she was just the normal, boring kid. Like she hadn't been enough.

Today at the store an old grandpa type had praised her, calling her "little mother." It had made her feel both grown-up and resentful, all at once.

Natalia loved her little brother. Of course she did. But a little baby needed a lot of attention. When he was brand-new, it had been rough. During the day he was fine, but that first year Conner barely slept at night. She and her parents endured endless hours of him red-faced and screaming. Which meant none of them slept.

Then one night: a miracle. The screaming stopped.

Natalia tiptoed into his room. Her parents were already there, staring down at his crib. Conner was in some state between sleeping and waking, sucking his thumb while the fingers of his free hand rubbed the satin binding of one of his million baby blankets. This one had been made by one of her mom's work friends. Plain yellow flannel on one side and green plaid on the other, it was bound together with a wide green strip of satin.

And from that night on, it was Conner's special blankie, the one thing he had to have to sleep or just calm down.

Most of the satin was now little more than dirty threads. Once, while Conner was napping, her mom had snuck it away and added new binding. When he woke up, he'd gotten so upset her mom had been forced to rip it back off.

Now Natalia's mom unlocked the door and pushed it open with her foot. She walked through the mudroom and set the bags down on the kitchen counter.

Natalia carried Conner inside. He had gotten cuter once he was finally able to talk. And asleep, he was always adorable, with his flushed cheeks, brown cowlick, and rosebud mouth.

"See if you can put him down without waking him up," her mom whispered.

Natalia tried not to jostle him as she started upstairs. Her feet made soft shushing sounds on the tan carpet. But he didn't stir as she laid him on his toddler bed, covered him with his blankie, and then gently closed the door.

Back downstairs, Natalia helped put things away. Her

mom suddenly muttered a swear word under her breath. "I can't believe it! I forgot the Parmesan."

"Do you have to have it?"

"It's like the main part of the recipe." Her mom frowned. "You can't have cacio e pepe without Parmesan."

Her mom was right. Without the salty, tangy strands of Parmesan tangling the pasta, it would just be starchy strings dotted with pepper. The pasta and a premade salad were supposed to be their dinner tonight. They had bought ingredients for other meals, but they all took much longer to cook.

They looked at each other. Natalia thought they were both picturing the same thing. Waking up a cranky Conner. His back arching, his face turning red. Trying to force him into his car seat. His ear-piercing screams as they drove back. Her mom would probably want Natalia to wait in the car with the doors locked while she ran in. Strangers would walk by, staring at her and the screaming toddler beside her.

"Why don't you just go back?" Natalia said. "Let him sleep, and I'll finish putting away the groceries."

"But you're not twelve yet." In Oregon, twelve was the age when a child could be left alone without an adult present. Natalia thought she and her mom were both looking forward to it, for different reasons.

"But I'll be twelve in six months." She straightened up, trying to look taller. "Besides, how long will it take? Ten minutes? I'll lock the doors. I have my cell phone. What can happen in ten minutes?"

"I don't know," her mom said slowly. But Natalia could

tell she was torn. Finally, she picked up her keys. "I'll be back in a flash."

After she left, Natalia felt so grown-up. Maybe if she demonstrated how capable she was, her mom would loosen up. After all, who cared that she was not exactly twelve? Just as long as she was able to handle things. And wouldn't her mom be happy if she came home and the pasta was already cooking?

Natalia ran the faucet until the water was as hot as it would get, then filled the big metal pot her mom always used. She already knew pasta tasted best if you cooked it in salted water, so she added several shakes. After setting it on the burner, she covered it with a lid, the way her mom did, so it would boil faster. Then she turned the knob on the gas stove all the way to the right, until it started making a clicking noise.

And she waited for the flame to flick on.

## CHAPTER 11

# THE COLOR OF BLOOD

10:03 P.M.

"HERE, I'LL TAKE HIM," a voice said. Hands started to pull the toddler from Natalia's arms.

With a start, she opened her eyes. Everyone was across the bridge now. It was an effort to relax her grip, to let go, to let Lisa take Trask. How long had she been standing there, eyes closed, half imagining she was holding her baby brother? Remembering a time that didn't exist anymore, except in her imagination?

"He's so relaxed with you," Lisa said as she guided Trask's dangling feet into the leg holes of his carrier. "Normally Trask doesn't like strangers. You must have a lot of experience babysitting."

"Actually, I don't." Natalia didn't elaborate. "He's probably just too tired to care."

Even more than fires, she had spent the last six years avoiding toddlers. If a family with a little kid came into the Dairy Barn, she always let one of her coworkers wait on them. And she would never, ever babysit.

Not that anyone who knew her would actually ask. Who would trust her?

People were taking sips of water or buckling up their

packs with stifled groans. Susan tucked her hat in her backpack and took out a headlamp. With the help of his own headlamp, Wyatt checked his map.

The sight of the headlamps reminded Natalia that she had also bought one at REI, in addition to the first aid kit. She dug it out, still in its packaging. *Oh crap*. It ran on batteries. Her panic was quickly followed by relief when she realized they were included. After opening the package, she pulled the band over her forehead. The moon was rising, but the huge disk the color of blood wasn't providing much light. Natalia knew the color was due to the smoke, but it still seemed like an evil portent.

They were in a small clearing. Marco shone his phone's flashlight on two carved signs nailed to a tree. One read, "Cougar Creek," and pointed to the left. The other read, "Twisted Trail," and pointed to the right.

Lisa looked up from the buckle she was snapping across Trask's chest. "Cougar Creek? Isn't that where the other fire is?" Her eyes were wide.

"Yeah." Wyatt looked up from his map. "So we definitely don't want to take that trail. Which leaves Twisted. The name's pretty accurate. It twists back and forth."

"How long until we get back to civilization?" Darryl rubbed Zion's drooping shoulders.

Wyatt pinched off distances with his fingers. "It's at least twenty miles before we connect up to another road."

*Twenty miles.* People exchanged shocked glances. They had already hiked two to Sky Bridge. This was going to be like completing a marathon, only on steep trails. At night.

With a fire at their back and the air hazy with smoke. By now Marco wasn't the only one coughing.

AJ made a face. "That will take forever."

"Probably all night." Wyatt folded up the map. "The average person hikes about two miles an hour. And that's in daylight and without an elevation change. Twisted is more of a, um, technically challenging trail."

Natalia wondered if she was the only one who noticed the hesitation in his words. Her stomach churned.

"But you can't really expect us to hike all night," Darryl objected.

"I'm not sure we have much choice, at least not right now. Maybe we can rest a little farther on. But we still need to put some distance between us and the fire."

"If that trail cuts back and forth, then why can't we just ignore it and use your compass to go in a straight line?" Ryan's face was drawn. "Wouldn't it be faster?"

Wyatt shook his head. "It might seem like it'd be faster, but by the time you climbed into and out of some slot canyons, forded a few streams, and bushwhacked your way through some heavy brush, it would take a lot longer than just staying on the trail." He looked back at the horizon, silhouetted by the fire. "My one worry is that the Cougar Creek fire could have spread all the way to Twisted. We don't want to get caught between that fire and the new one."

"That sign said *Trail closed due to fire*," Beatriz said, tying her beach towel around her shoulders like a cape. "It didn't say *trails*."

Basing a decision on the lack of an *s* on a hastily scrawled sign did not seem like the best idea. Natalia pictured the two fires curling around them like the fingers of a fist. And then the fist squeezing closed. When she tried to swallow, her tongue felt like a piece of leather.

"I don't think we have any choice." Marco pointed at the flames, creeping ever closer. "One blown spark and the fire could jump the canyon."

Natalia's dread was expanding to include anything and everything. In addition to the fire, she was also afraid of the dark. Of tripping or slipping again, only this time really getting hurt. Afraid of getting lost. Of being abandoned. Of wild animals. Of deep water. Of watching someone get hurt and being unable to help.

*Five things you can see*, she told herself.

But the first thing she saw was Trask, rubbing his eyes, his little mouth bunched into a frown. She couldn't look at him, and she couldn't stop looking at him. Even so, she helped Lisa lift Trask's carrier onto Wyatt's back.

They had just set off into the cover of the trees when AJ abruptly stopped.

"Wait a minute." His head swiveled back and forth. "Where's Susan?"

## CHAPTER 12

# WHATEVER DOES KILL YOU

10:14 P.M.

**"DID SUSAN EVEN MAKE** it over the bridge?" Ryan asked.

"Yeah. She was ahead of me." Marco scanned the murky darkness.

"So she's got to be nearby," AJ said. "She doesn't move that fast. Maybe she just went off to pee or something." He cupped his hands over his mouth. "Susan! Susan! Where are you?"

The others joined in. After locating her whistle, Natalia gave several short blasts. Then Wyatt held up his hand, gesturing for silence. The only sound was the distant crackle of flames and the churning rush of the water at the bottom of the canyon. The horizon behind them was silhouetted by the fire, turning some trees along the ridgeline into black cardboard cutouts and others blazing torches. Not only was the fire moving toward them, but it was also spreading out.

Deep inside herself, Natalia just wanted to run away into the darkness. Or lie down and curl up, tighter and tighter, until she disappeared. How long could they even afford to look for Susan?

"We can't leave her behind," Beatriz said. "She'll die."

Jason made an impatient noise. "This one-for-all-and-all-for-one crap is going to end up meaning we all die."

To Natalia's surprise, Darryl agreed. "Jason's not one hundred percent wrong. We can't afford to hang around here for too long." The fire reflected on his sunglasses, making it hard to read his expression.

"I hate to say it," Lisa said, "but hasn't she seemed confused?"

"She asked me if anyone had a hand clock," Natalia admitted. "I think she meant a watch."

"My grandma says things like that," Zion volunteered. People turned to stare. It was the first time Natalia had heard him speak. "She has Alzheimer's. Sometimes she forgets words or uses the wrong ones. And sometimes she runs off and hides." As his grandson spoke, Darryl bowed his head.

Letting go of Darryl's hand, Zion walked over to the dog. "Hey, maybe Blue can find her!" He bent forward. "Blue, find Susan! Find Susan, Blue!"

It was true that the two had seemed drawn to each other. Blue tilted his head. For a second, everyone stared at the dog as he stared back at the boy.

Marco put his hand on top of the dog's head. "Look, Blue's one of the greatest dogs I know, but he's not some special breed trained to perform amazing tasks. He's just husky mixed with pit bull and maybe a little German shepherd. He probably doesn't even know what you're saying."

"How about this?" Wyatt offered. "I'll look for her.

The rest of you go on ahead and then the two of us will catch up with you."

Beatriz shook her head. "You're the one who was saying we shouldn't get separated."

"Beatriz is right," AJ said. "And you're the only one who really understands how to get us out of here."

Wyatt sighed. "Everyone's right. We can't leave Susan, but we also can't afford to stay here. Let's spend just ten minutes looking for her. The fire can't make that much progress in ten minutes. And if we don't find her, then we'll leave a note on the bridge."

No one objected to his plan. The fire made it clear they didn't have time to debate.

Darryl, Zion, and a half-asleep Trask were left in front of the bridge. Zion wanted to join the search, but was persuaded his grandpa needed him. Wyatt gave Darryl Natalia's whistle, with instructions to blow it after ten minutes. Then the rest of them fanned out. The dark was lit up with the bobbing lights of Wyatt's and Natalia's headlamps and the others' phones.

Natalia took the edge of canyon, but this time she kept about thirty feet away. Alone in the dark, her fears came crowding back. What if someone really *had* pushed her earlier? After all, she didn't know any of these people except Wyatt. What if someone was following her now? In the dark, they could do anything with no witnesses.

Behind her, a stick cracked.

With a shriek, Natalia whirled around but saw no one. The cone of light cast by her headlamp just lit up millions of smoke particles right in front of her, floating like flecks of dust. Her imagination was clearly getting the better of her. Putting her hand on her chest above her racing heart, she ordered herself to focus on finding Susan.

"Susan!" she shouted through cupped hands as she turned back. "Susan!" Farther away the same call echoed from other mouths. But what if Susan had forgotten more than words? What if she had forgotten her own name?

It was hard to see through the smoke. As an experiment, Natalia flicked the switch on her headlamp to off. The fire cast enough light that she could still see. It was like walking in a red-tinged twilight. She made sure to stay well away from the drop.

Every strange noise still made her start, in the hope that it was Susan, in the fear it was someone else. The space between her shoulder blades was itching, like someone was watching her. The sensation grew stronger and stronger, but each time she spun around, there was no one there. They were all searching in the same general area, she reminded herself. Any strange noises weren't strange at all, just another member of the group.

As Natalia's eyes began to adapt, she picked out more details: a tree trunk, a bush, a patch of ferns. A line of silver on the ground caught her eye. It was one of Susan's trekking poles. She picked it up. "Susan! Susan, where are you?" A few feet farther on, she found the second. Why had she discarded them? With a jolt of fear, Natalia thought of the drop to the water, far below. Was the reason they couldn't find Susan because she was no longer here to be found?

But then she caught a glimpse of something lighter

than its surroundings. "Susan?" She squinted. The older woman stood tucked inside a small, gnarled tree, nearly hidden by the branches. She had switched off her headlamp. Only her pale face gave her away.

Turning back, Natalia cupped her hands around her mouth. "I found Susan! She's okay!" Then she beckoned the older woman. "Come on out!"

After a moment's hesitation, Susan squeezed through the branches, scratching her arms in the process.

"Careful, Susan!" Natalia swiped at the beaded blood on Susan's skin with the tissue Wyatt had advised her to save.

The older woman lifted her chin. "Honey, you're the one who should be careful. We aren't alone."

Natalia's blood chilled. "What do you mean?"

"I saw . . ." Susan's voice trailed off. She gestured behind Natalia.

Natalia whirled around again, but all she saw were the lights of the other searchers bobbing toward them. Turning back, she grabbed Susan's arm. "What did you see?"

But now Susan was looking down at her bloody scratches. "What happened to my arms?"

Wyatt hurried up, followed by the other searchers. He hugged both of them, but Natalia's hug lasted quite a bit longer. Long enough that she almost forgot about her fear and Susan's confusion.

When he let go, she said, "Susan was just taking a little break." It was too embarrassing to bring up the older woman's confusion right in front of her. Natalia returned the trekking poles to Susan.

Back at the bridge, they set off down Twisted Trail. Once they were among the trees, it was too dark for Natalia to rely on her night vision. She snapped her head-lamp back on and tried to see past the eddying smoke. While the trees sheltered them from seeing the worst of the flames, they did nothing to block the snapping and crackling at their backs. It almost sounded like the fire was breathing.

The smoke was irritating her eyes, and she had to keep wiping them. Her boots felt as heavy as boulders. She really had to pee, but she was trying to ignore the urge.

Wyatt fell into step beside her.

"Tell me again," she said. "Why do you think this hiking thing is so great?"

"I like getting in touch with nature." He gave her a lopsided grin that was almost enough to distract her from the suffocating feeling of the trees pressing up against the trail, the thought of the fire at their backs.

"*In touch with*? This is more like getting mauled. You do realize mankind has spent literally thousands of years thinking up ways to get further away from nature?"

"Okay. Then I like challenging myself." He steadied her with a hand under her elbow. "Remember what Nietzsche said. 'Whatever doesn't kill us makes us stronger.'"

Natalia snorted. "The corollary is: 'Whatever *does* kill you makes you dead.'"

"I like a girl who knows the word *corollary*." Wyatt gave her elbow a squeeze and then let go.

"It's a little late for flattery." Still, flirting helped her forget the deadly reality for a few moments.

"I'll try anything if you'll just forgive me." His tone turned serious. "I know I got you into this mess. I promise I'll get you out."

"It's okay," she said. He clearly meant it, but would meaning it be enough?

As they trudged farther down Twisted Trail, conversations dwindled to silence, except for Marco's continual light cough. Every now and then Zion would whisper an instruction to guide his grandfather around an obstacle. Occasionally the trail tacked in a different direction for no reason Natalia could see except to give Twisted Trail its name. Every now and then she surreptitiously checked the time on her phone. Still zero bars. Soon it would technically be a new day.

The trees thinned out and the path started to rise, rocky and steep. Her thighs burned. She could tell the red spot on her toe had become a blister.

A distant rumble began to fill the air. She tilted her head, trying to identify the sound.

And then they turned for a switchback, and she saw what was making the noise. The path led directly to a waterfall.

Natalia grabbed Wyatt's arm. "What are we going to do? The trail just ends."

"You just can't see it. That's Hideaway Falls. It's called that because you actually hike behind the waterfall."

Normally, that information alone would have been

enough to make her freak out, to worry about slippery rocks, about falling into the thundering white water. But now she had eyes only for the narrow trail leading to the falls. It had been carved into the middle of what was basically a cliff. One side was just a rocky wall.

The other was a straight drop a hundred feet down.

## CHAPTER 13

# A FLASH OF SILVER

11:37 P.M.

EVERYONE CAME TO A stop, staring at the faint line of the trail that hugged the cliff face and then disappeared under the thundering falls.

"What's wrong?" Darryl swiveled his head blindly.

"The path ahead is really high up, Grandpa," Zion answered. "Like on a cliff. And there's nothing to stop us from falling off."

Ryan grimaced. "The trail also goes behind a waterfall. It's going to be like walking on the lip of a glass—while it's being filled up."

Lisa poked a finger at Wyatt. "Did you know about this back when we started on Twisted?"

He sighed. "What good would it have done if I'd told you guys? It's not exactly like we have a choice. This is the way we have to go if we want to escape the fire. Besides, there's a cable set into the wall you can hold on to."

Even Jason look daunted. "Dude, there's got to be another way. Didn't you say we could bushwhack if we had to?"

Wyatt pointed into the darkness. "There's a river down there. And it's a long way down on nothing but scree—those small loose rocks. Even if we managed to get to the bottom without spraining an ankle, we'd have to cross the river. The river's still running high with snow melt, so we'd have to swim." Wyatt didn't need to spell it out. Would Zion get swept up by the current? What about Ryan, already weakened by his burns? "And we'd have to leave our stuff behind. People have drowned when they tried to swim with their packs on."

"I say we stick to the trail," Susan said. Then she glanced down, and her certainty evaporated. "Wait, what happened to my arms?" Her fingers traced the scratches she had gotten from hiding.

"You got caught up in a tree," Natalia said, biting her lip so she wouldn't add, "remember?" Because it was clear the older woman didn't.

They started off. Wyatt was in the lead and Jason in the rear. Natalia was somewhere in the middle, between Darryl and Beatriz. With each step, the trail got higher and narrower, until it was basically a five-foot-wide shelf on the side of a cliff. She was careful to look only a few feet ahead, her headlamp illuminating just the path, which followed the natural curves and folds of the cliff.

Wyatt had to shout to be heard over the waterfall. He raised his left hand above his head and waggled it to get their attention. "Here's the cable." He reached down and grabbed it.

When Natalia reached the cable, she clamped on so tightly she could feel the individual strands of metal that had been twisted together to form it. It was hard to let herself loosen her grip enough to move forward.

Ahead of her, people began to chant. Once she understood the words, she joined in. "Keep to the left, hold the cable." Her feet fell into rhythm with the words. "Keep to the left, hold the cable."

With the others, Natalia crept along the trail, only releasing the cable each time she needed to slip past an eye bolt set into the rocks. On one side, the cable and the rough cliff wall. On the other, nothing but air and a fall that would surely kill her. She hugged the near edge so tightly that her left shoulder kept scraping against randomly protruding rocks.

The night, she slowly realized, was actually her friend. Because of it, she couldn't see the rocks or the water far below. She was only imagining them. Even with the fire behind them, if it had been daylight, she might have refused to attempt this. But if she was careful to focus on the physical details of what was right in front of her, the way Dr. Paris had taught her, her fears would stay imaginary.

Natalia mentally cataloged sensory details to keep herself from getting lost in what-ifs. In the light of her headlamp, her eyes picked out a tiny tree somehow managing to grow from the side of the cliff. Darryl's gnarled hand on the cable. Past Darryl, a glimpse of Zion's tight curls.

The one relief was the air was less smoky here. She took deep breaths, enjoying the clean taste of it. As they got closer to the waterfall, tiny drops of cold water freckled her face.

The trail curved to the left. At the same time the edge of the cliff started to curl above them, until it was a seamless curve forming both wall and ceiling. Ahead of them, the falls fell past the trail like a curtain.

"Keep to the left, hold the cable. Keep to the left, hold the cable." In order to be heard above the thundering water, they were now half shouting. Something about hearing her voice twining with all the others made Natalia feel stronger.

Walking behind the waterfall was like entering a cave. Behind her, Jason played the light of his phone over their surroundings. The glistening rock roof was a few feet above their heads. To their right was a thick curtain of gray-and-white water. Its thunder was all she could hear. The air was saturated with droplets that sparkled in the phone's light. It was like being sprayed by a giant plant mister.

Once they were out of the falls. Natalia began to relax. The roar slowly faded. The path was starting to slope downward. Eventually they would reach the bottom. The worst was over. They had made it through unscathed.

Then behind her, almost drowned out by the falls, she heard a faint cry. There was a flash of silver in her peripheral vision as Beatriz's duct tape shoe flew up in the air.

Without thinking, Natalia released the cable and turned. She reached out and managed to grab Beatriz's right wrist as she slipped off the path. The sudden jerk of the other girl's weight almost yanked her over, but then Marco caught Beatriz's other wrist.

But Beatriz was still dangling in darkness, with nothing under her feet.

Natalia gritted her teeth and bent her knees in a half

squat. Beatriz's weight was inexorably pulling her forward. Her hiking boots found little purchase on the slick rocks. Blue was barking, but everyone else had stopped moving, stopped chanting.

But then Darryl's hands clamped below hers on Beatriz's wrist. Together, the three of them pulled Beatriz back onto the trail. She landed on her belly, then pushed herself to her hands and knees. Her chest was heaving. Marco threw himself down next to her and began to stroke her hair, murmuring into her ear.

Straightening up, Natalia put her back flat against the cliff wall. She was shaking so hard she felt like she might fall apart. Around her, people's faces were still distorted with shock. Wyatt squeezed past everyone to hug her. She was finally relaxing against his strong chest, when Lisa's angry voice interrupted.

"What the hell, Wyatt! Did you even think about how you've got Trask on your back?" she demanded. "What if you had lost your balance just so you could give your girlfriend a hug? Then both of you could have—" Grimacing, she put her hands over her mouth and took a step back. Abruptly, she tipped sideways.

With a cry, she dropped into the dark.

## CHAPTER 14

# EVERY BREATH

SIX YEARS EARLIER

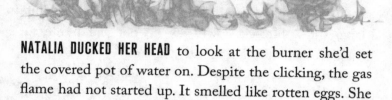

**NATALIA DUCKED HER HEAD** to look at the burner she'd set the covered pot of water on. Despite the clicking, the gas flame had not started up. It smelled like rotten eggs. She twisted the knob to the off position.

Her mom had complained about this burner before. But what exactly did she do when it wouldn't light? Then Natalia remembered. There was a box of wooden matches on the top shelf of the cupboard, kept as far away from Conner as possible.

The flame of the first match went out when Natalia tried to move it toward the stove. The second died before she even turned the knob. The third time she turned the knob before she scraped the match along the rough brown stripe on the outside of the box. It took three tries before it caught.

*Woof!* A ball of orange exploded in front of her. The right cuff of her long-sleeved shirt caught fire. She watched it race up her arm like a magic trick she didn't understand.

She had to run for the sink, her arm a torch in front of her. Every step fed more air to the flames. As she turned on the faucet, the fire from her sleeve caught the muslin curtains framing the kitchen window. It raced up one side and then leapt onto the wallboard and found a foothold. It expanded as it burned, making a V shape on the white-painted wall as it made its way to the ceiling.

Meanwhile, Natalia's sleeve was still burning. She leaned forward to get the full length of her sleeve under the blast of water. She finally succeeded in dousing the flames on her shirt, but the fire no longer needed her. Bits of burning curtain landed on a dish towel and an open cookbook. Then the cupboard over the cookbook started to burn, as well as the cardboard boxes inside it, and the cereal, crackers, and cookies inside the boxes. Overhead the smoke alarm buzzed like a mosquito, barely audible over the hungry roar of the fire.

She turned. The stovetop itself was on fire, fed by oily residue in the burner wells.

A glass sat on the countertop. Natalia grabbed it and stuck it under the faucet. Even before it was full, she was throwing its contents. She put out a few of the flames, but the fire kept spreading. It had reached the ceiling now, rolling overhead and doubling in size every minute.

Suddenly she remembered she had more to worry about than just herself. Conner was upstairs. She dropped the glass in the sink and ran.

By the time she reached the stairs, the hot cloud of black smoke had thickened and deepened. It inched down to the top of the kitchen doorway, then quickly streamed out of the room, traveling through the hall and following her up the stairway. By the time she reached his bedroom door, smoke was pooling around her ankles.

As she swung it open, the fire leapt on the fresh oxygen. The backdraft knocked her to the floor. Gasping for breath, she took in only bitter fumes. Gagging, she crawled across the carpet. Her one thought was to save Conner.

But when she reached his bed, it was empty. Empty! How could that be? She frantically ran her hands over the rumpled covers, searching for him by touch as much as sight. Thick black choking smoke was filling the room.

And then she thought to look under the bed. She dropped to her belly. And there he was, absolutely still, eyes wide, clutching his blankie.

She reached out, grabbed his small arm, and dragged him out. He was nearly limp, and she didn't know if it was from the smoke or sheer, primal terror. In order to carry him, she had to stand up. Stand up into the dark, choking smoke. Clutching him to her chest, she staggered blindly toward his bedroom window. When she raised it, the air gave the flames another boost. Ashes and smoke blew past her as the fire was sucked toward the fresh supply of oxygen.

Behind her was the fire, now racing into the room. Below her was a fifteen-foot drop to the concrete driveway. She pushed out the screen and heard it clatter when it landed.

Natalia's only thought was for her brother. Every breath was searing her lungs. His were so much smaller. She grabbed Conner's wrists and then lowered him out the window so he could breathe. He finally made a sound, a wordless protest when his blankie fell onto the driveway.

She inched forward until her hip bones rested on top of the sill. It was as far as she could go.

Conner dangled from her hands. Behind her, his bedroom was now on fire. The house was on fire. It felt like the whole world was on fire. A chunk of burning ceiling landed on Natalia's thigh. She had no way of getting it off, not without risking her brother's life. It didn't even hurt that much.

At least not at first.

Her grip did not loosen. There was nothing underneath Conner to break his fall. Not a tree or a bush. Not even a patch of grass. Just the unforgiving asphalt of the driveway.

The smoke billowing from behind her was so thick she could no longer see Conner dangling from her hands. He wasn't twisting or moving. He was now absolutely still. Was he still breathing? Was he even conscious?

"Help!" she screamed into the blackness. "Help us!"

But there was no answer. Next to her, the windows in her parents' bedroom suddenly blew out. A piece of glass sliced her chin as flames shot out.

Half her body was outside the window. The heat and smoke behind her were pushing her farther out.

No one was coming. If she did nothing, she would burn to death and he would fall. The only possible way to save him was to bring him back inside, clutch him to her chest and throw herself back out of the window, hoping that her body would cushion him. That she would absorb the force of the fall.

She adjusted her grip, getting ready to haul him back

up. And suddenly, Conner came to life. It was like trying to clutch a twisting fish.

She tried to hold on to his wrists. Then his hands. Then his fingers.

Then Conner was gone.

And Natalia pushed herself out into the air after him.

## CHAPTER 15

# NOTHING BUT DARKNESS

12:22 A.M.

**EVERYONE WAS STARING AT** the space where Lisa should have been. Some people were screaming. Ryan's mouth was so wide Natalia could see the glint of fillings, but he was silent, his empty hands reaching out to the empty air that had once held his wife.

Lisa had dropped off the trail at a point where the path pinched down. Falling to her knees, Natalia army-crawled forward until her head hung over the edge.

Her headlamp shone on Lisa's body. But it wasn't a hundred feet down, broken on boulders. She was just ten feet below them, precariously cradled in a steeply slanted cleft barely wide enough for her body. She lay on her back, her right leg bent. Three feet past Lisa's left foot was nothing but darkness.

Wyatt hurriedly handed the child carrier to Marco and dropped on the dirt next to Natalia.

As Natalia watched, one of Lisa's hands twitched. She was alive!

But there was no time to rejoice. Lisa began to scream. Her hands went to her right knee. As she writhed in pain, she slid an inch closer to the edge.

"Stay still, Lisa!" Natalia shouted. "Don't move!"

"My knee! My knee!" Her voice was choked with tears.

"We're going to help you," Wyatt called. "But right now you cannot move or you'll slide off!"

On his knees and one unbandaged hand, Ryan crawled toward the edge.

Natalia could see two Lisas. The one lying on her back. The other, the one in her imagination, sliding off in a skitter of pebbles.

Natalia called, "Lisa! What's wrong with your knee?" So many blood vessels ran through the joint. A broken bone could become a knife. Even if they could get Lisa back up on the trail, Natalia couldn't fix a severed vein or artery.

"It just"—Lisa panted between words—"gave out . . . all of a sudden." She groaned, and then arched her back so she could look up at Wyatt. "Where's Trask?"

"Marco's got him, honey," Ryan called out. "Be careful!"

"Can you turn over and crawl toward us?" Natalia asked.

"I don't know." Slowly, Lisa started to flip over but then rolled back with a shriek. "I can't. I can't move my knee at all." Her voice was shaky with tears and panic.

"You guys have got to help her!" Ryan said urgently.

"Do you have a rope?" Natalia asked Wyatt. "If we made a loop and Lisa put it under her arms, we could haul her back up."

Wyatt bit his lip. "All I've got is some parachute cord. It's strong, but it's not nearly thick enough. It would be like trying to drag her up with a piece of twine."

"Take Blue's leash!" Marco called out.

As it passed from hand to hand, Jason said, "Even if you get Lisa back up here, what happens then? If her knee's broken, she won't be able to walk."

Ryan's head whipped around. "Shut up! No one cares what you think."

But Jason was right. If Lisa couldn't walk, then what? Could they improvise a stretcher with Susan's trekking poles?

But first they had to get her up. Holding the padded handle, Wyatt dropped the leash down. It was too short. The end landed about four feet above Lisa's head. And even if she could reach it, how could she use it if she couldn't even move her leg?

Natalia thought of SAMPLE. Most of it didn't apply. But now she seized on the *P—Pertinent history.*

"Lisa! Has this ever happened before?"

"Once. In high school." She spoke through gritted teeth. "I was playing basketball and my knee just collapsed. Dislocated kneecap. It felt like this."

Hope surged in Natalia. "And how did they treat it?"

"Just pushed it back into place while they pulled my leg straight." She panted. "It hurt worse than having a baby."

Lisa's cropped pants ended at her calf.

"Can you do something for me?" Natalia said. "Can you pull up that one pant leg so I can see your knee?"

With a grimace, Lisa grabbed the cloth at the thigh and edged it upward until her knee was exposed. Even from ten feet away it was obviously misshapen. Instead of being in front, the circle of the patella was now on the outside edge of her knee. It looked like someone had tucked an egg under the skin.

"Okay, Lisa," Wyatt called. "I'm going to come down there and try to put your kneecap back in place."

Natalia's stomach dropped at the thought. She pitched her voice for his ears alone. "That space is barely big enough to hold her. You could both go over the edge."

"No, Wyatt. It's not safe," Lisa said. She had either heard Natalia or had the same thought. "I think I can do it myself."

"Are you sure, honey?" Ryan called. "Maybe let Wyatt try."

"I'll try it myself first." Lisa's voice shook but she sounded certain.

"Won't that hurt a lot?" Wyatt asked Natalia in a low voice.

"Either way it's going to hurt a lot." She pictured the anatomy and then raised her voice. "Okay, use your left hand to massage the muscles on the outside of your right thigh. That's your quadriceps, and it attaches to the kneecap. Try to get it to relax. Then take the heel of your right hand and as you straighten your leg, push the kneecap back into place."

Groaning through gritted teeth, Lisa started to massage her thigh. She set her other hand next to the skewed kneecap, then began to straighten her right leg. But her foot hadn't gone more than an inch when she stopped. "I can't," she panted. "It hurts so much."

"You can do it, Lisa," Ryan said. "Do it for Trask!"

Lisa put her hands into position again. She started making a high-pitched keening noise. It sounded almost like she was singing, holding a single note that stretched out endlessly. But as she massaged and straightened and pressed, the egg-shaped bump slid over and popped into place. The sound she was making abruptly ended with an audible sigh of relief.

The entire procedure had taken less than thirty seconds.

"Can you move it now?" Natalia asked.

Lisa tentatively bent and then straightened her knee, stopping when she began to slide downhill. "I think so." Her voice shook. "But how am I going to get back up?"

"Now that you can move your leg, you just need to get to the leash," Wyatt said. "I think if you very carefully turn over onto your stomach there will be less risk of you sliding." Natalia held her breath as Lisa carefully did. "There, that's it. Now see if you can crawl farther away from the edge."

Step by step, Wyatt, with encouragement from Ryan, coached Lisa as she half crawled, half dragged herself nearer to them and farther away from the edge. Finally she got close enough to grab the leash.

"Now hold on tight, get to your feet, and go up hand over hand like it's a climbing rope."

"Be careful, honey," Susan called as Lisa slowly began to pull herself up. She was putting weight on her right leg, albeit gingerly. The muscles in Wyatt's arms bulged as he held her steady.

Finally with a grunt and a heave, Lisa was back on the

trail. She turned so she was parallel with it and then lay on her back, panting. Ryan knelt next to her, stroking her forehead.

Natalia knelt on the other side. Lisa's pant leg was still rolled up, exposing her knee. The kneecap was in the right place and it didn't even look swollen. "I'm going to touch your knee, okay?"

"Yeah."

She palpated gently, but felt no sharp edges, only dampness. Lisa's skin was covered by a light layer of sweat. "How does it feel?"

"A lot better. But not completely normal."

Natalia looked up at the other woman's face. "Do you think you could walk?"

Lisa raised one dark eyebrow. "Do I have a choice?"

What Lisa needed was a brace, like a person might wear after knee surgery. Natalia's eyes lit on Marco's backpack, which he had given to Beatriz. "Marco, do you think I could borrow your backpack and empty it out?"

"Sure." He began to transfer snacks and sunscreen from his pack to Wyatt's.

Natalia pointed. "Oh, can I have that T-shirt, too?"

"It's not very clean."

"I just want to use it for padding." After undoing the backpack straps, she wrapped it around the knee, padding the bend with Marco's T-shirt. Then she refastened the straps in front, tightening them until the pack was firmly holding the knee.

"There." Natalia got to her feet and held out her hand. "Let's see what it feels like when you walk on it."

With the brace preventing her from bending, it took some effort for Lisa to get on her feet. But once she was up, she took a step, and then another. A smile lightened her face. "That feels a lot better."

Ryan hugged her with his good arm. She closed her eyes and leaned forward so that their foreheads touched.

There was one more thing that would help. Natalia called to Susan. "Is it okay if Lisa uses one of your trekking poles?"

Susan looked at her with rheumy eyes. "What? Who are you?"

AJ patted her shoulder. "It's Natalia, Susan. Can I give her one of your poles to help Lisa?" When the older woman nodded, he gave it to her.

Lisa put it in her right hand, but then Natalia put it in her left. "Actually you use it on the opposite side of the injury. That way you'll plant it at the same time you're putting weight on your bad leg."

Wyatt already had Trask on his back. The toddler had been roused by all the noise but now was nodding off again, opening and closing his palms. "I think we should get going as soon as you think you can."

Natalia allowed herself to look back. The sky was red from one end to the other with flames.

Lisa lifted her chin. "Let's do it."

## CHAPTER 16

# SUFFOCATING

SIX YEARS EARLIER

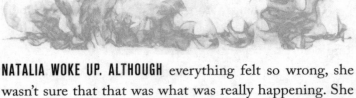

NATALIA WOKE UP. ALTHOUGH everything felt so wrong, she wasn't sure that that was what was really happening. She couldn't even summon the energy to open her eyes. Maybe she was still having a dream. A nightmare. Where was she? She wasn't even exactly sure *who* she was.

Something plastic had been pushed past her lips and jammed down her throat. There was no word for what it felt like. Like she was suffocating, but also like she had put her head out the window of a speeding car and opened her mouth wide. Every few seconds, the noisy hiss changed in a two-note rhythm. *Whoosh-whoosh.* And each time, the thing down her throat twitched.

One thought filled her mind. *Get it out!* She began to scrabble at whatever was stuffed in her mouth, but her hands felt stiff and oddly muffled. Forcing open her swollen lids, she saw she was lying on a white bed in a white room. Her hands were also white—splinted and wrapped in thick layers of bandages until they were as useful as fat white paddles. Still, she tried again to dislodge the foreign thing choking her.

Someone grabbed her wrists. "It's okay, Natalia," a stranger's voice said. A woman. "You're safe."

*Natalia.* That was her name. Everything came back in a rush. She remembered flinging herself after her brother when he had twisted himself from her hands. But when she tried to ask about Conner, she realized she couldn't make a sound, not even a groan.

The woman patted her shoulder. "I'm afraid you won't be able to talk for a bit. We had to put a tube down your throat to give you oxygen and medicine and to keep your airway from swelling closed."

This had to be a hospital. Conner must be in another room.

Natalia remembered somersaulting forward. Time had slowed. The air was filled with black acrid smoke. She could not see Conner. But below her there was a sound like a slap. Her body kept turning. Just as she passed the living room window, it shattered. Shards of glass and balls of fire shot past her.

Screaming Conner's name, Natalia somehow landed on her feet. Instantly, one of her ankles snapped and she tumbled forward. But it was as if it was happening to someone else. She felt nothing. Not the burns, not the broken bone.

She had become a ghost, hovering above it all. And then it was as if she had flickered out of existence.

Only now Natalia was back. She had survived, after all. But what about Conner? She began to thrash, desperate to say his name. Desperate to hear it. To hear him.

The nurse was still talking, but about nothing Natalia cared about. "You breathed in a lot of smoke and gases, but we should be able to remove the breathing tube in a day or two." Her voice became a falsely cheerful lilt. "Your parents are going to be so glad to hear you're awake."

It felt like one of those nightmares where you try to run but your feet find no purchase. Where was Conner? Natalia ripped one hand free from the nurse's and began to hit the bed. Why wasn't the nurse telling her the most important thing?

But part of her kept replaying the sound she'd heard before she landed. Like a slap.

"I'm just going to give you a little something in your IV to help you sleep, Natalia. To help you heal."

Slowly, Natalia stopped fussing. When the darkness came, she welcomed it. Her last thought was of her little brother's chubby hands.

An hour or a day or a week later, she woke up again. When she forced her eyes open, her parents were sitting next to the bed. They were dressed in clothes she had never seen before, ill-fitting and wrinkled. The skin around their eyes looked bruised. They started up when they saw she was awake.

The breathing tube was still in her mouth. But when her mom looked in Natalia's eyes, she saw her question.

"I'm so sorry, honey." And then her mom was ugly-crying, snot and tears streaming down her red face. "I killed Conner, and I thought I'd killed you, too."

Natalia twisted her head from side to side. Her mom wasn't guilty of anything. It was Natalia's fault. All of it.

Her fault for urging her mother to go back to the store. Her fault for persisting in trying to light the stove. Her fault for not getting to her brother sooner, or figuring out how to safely get him out. Couldn't she have tied a bed-sheet under his arms and then tied that to another sheet and lowered him to the ground?

She wanted her parents to scream at her. To tell her she was not their daughter anymore. Even though her dad didn't say anything, didn't do much more than bite his lip and look at the floor, she could tell he didn't blame her, either.

Which was almost worse.

"I should have gotten that burner fixed," her mom continued in a high, strangled-sounding voice. "I should have guessed you would try to help me by starting the pasta water. The fire captain told me modern houses have so many things made of plastic and chemicals that they burn really fast. He said that, thirty years ago, if your house caught on fire, you still had fifteen minutes to get out. Now you're lucky if you have three."

~

Two days later, Natalia was in surgery. The worst of the burned skin on the back of her legs was surgically removed and replaced with a thin layer of healthy skin harvested from her inner thighs. The remaining burns had to be frequently scrubbed to remove dead and dying tissue. Even on painkillers, it was agony. She spent a total of six days on the burn unit, three of them on a ventilator. Days after it was removed, she was still coughing up black mucus. Her days in the hospital were filled with dressing changes, physical therapy, occupational therapy, and as much sleep as she could manage.

Only sleep offered her a reprieve from the terrible reality. Not only was Conner dead, but she slowly figured out their whole house was gone. Their clothes. Books. Appliances. Furniture. Photos of her dead grandmother. Letters from her great-great-great-grandparents. All turned to ash.

On the seventh day, she went home to heal. Only there was no home. Just an apartment filled with hastily purchased IKEA furniture and an odd assortment of stuff people called donations but really seemed like things they just wanted to get rid of.

There were still two months left in the school year, but Natalia didn't go back to fifth grade. She couldn't. In fact, she couldn't go out in public at all. Burns were basically like open wounds, the doctors said, putting her at high risk for infection. The skin was the biggest organ of the body, they told her. It was responsible for keeping the fluid in her body, while keeping out bacteria and viruses. It also helped a person maintain a steady internal temperature.

Natalia also knew that your skin was the first thing people saw when they looked at you. And it allowed you to touch. To feel things.

Only she was determined to feel nothing. If you felt things, if you cared about people, then you could get hurt. She couldn't help caring about her parents, but she withdrew from her friends and was careful not to make new ones. She wasn't rude, not exactly. Just detached.

For most of sixth grade, Natalia had to wear compression shorts under her clothes to try to smooth the scars on the backs of her thighs. It only partly worked. The skin there still healed tighter and rougher, the texture and color different from the soft white skin around it. The scars looked like she felt. Like she was the rougher, uglier person surrounded by other people with soft, easy lives. People who had no idea how quickly everything could go wrong. How you could lose it all. Lose it all in a heartbeat.

## CHAPTER 17

# STOP, THINK, OBSERVE, PLAN
1:43 A.M.

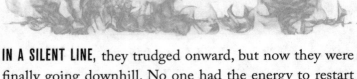

**IN A SILENT LINE,** they trudged onward, but now they were finally going downhill. No one had the energy to restart the chant about holding on to the cable.

Natalia's toe, which earlier had been burning, now felt wet. The blister must have broken. But it was silly to pay any attention to a toe when Ryan and Lisa must be suffering far more. She had given them pain pills from her dwindling supply, but over-the-counter medications could not make up for the fact that they both needed rest and a real doctor.

Gradually the sounds of Hideaway Falls faded, replaced by the huff of labored breathing, the scuff of feet, and the faint grumble of the flames behind them. Marco kept up his steady, light cough.

Eventually, the trail widened so it was no longer just a narrow edge cut into the side of a cliff. The terrain began to flatten out, the rocks giving way to bushes and even small trees. Now if someone missed a step, they wouldn't fall to their death. They reached the last stretch of cable. After Natalia let go, she had to massage the cramped fingers of her left hand. They felt as if they were permanently shaped into hooks.

She slid her phone from her pocket. Still no service. It was nearly two in the morning. They had been hiking six hours. It felt like forever.

Once the trail widened, Wyatt began again to walk up and down the line. He checked in with folks, joked around, but still kept everyone moving. Natalia realized that he did something similar during rushes at the Dairy Barn. Until today she hadn't appreciated how vital his efforts were to keeping things running smoothly.

As Wyatt fell back into step with her, he reached for her hand without saying anything. For a moment, the press of his warm, calloused fingers made her forget about everything else. She wondered what it would be like to kiss Wyatt. The thought even took her mind off Trask. He was regarding her dully, his eyes at half-mast.

Ahead of them, the trail curved. When Natalia and Wyatt rounded the bend, the people at the head of the line had come to a halt. Wyatt let go of her hand and went forward to see what was wrong.

A tree had snapped at the base and fallen across the trail. The light from her headlamp traced the trunk, which was a little bigger around than a telephone pole. At the roots, where it had splintered, was a black, rotting spot. The tree's crown was propped up by the branches. The top edge of the trunk was about waist-high and the bottom edge ended about two feet above the ground. Wyatt leaned his full weight on it and gave it a shove, but it didn't budge.

Too tired even to debate what to do, some people started clambering over while others crawled under. Deciding she would rather start on the ground than fall onto it, Natalia opted for the latter. First she pushed her pack through, then went under herself. Rough bark scraped the top of her head, and the metallic scent of earth filled her nostrils. The glow of her headlamp picked out the scrapes on her hands, the dirt rimming her fingernails. She had cleared the trunk and was about to stand up when a cracking and groaning noise to her left jolted her with panic. She threw herself forward.

And then AJ screamed. When Natalia turned back, he was flat on his belly, his hands pushing his backpack in front of him, and the trunk resting on his lower back and hips.

And there was no space between them. Whatever branches had been holding up the trunk must have snapped.

Natalia dropped to her knees next to AJ. "Do you feel like anything's broken?"

"I don't know." His voice shook. "I don't think so. It feels more like pressure than pain."

"That's good," she said in cheerful voice. She had no idea if it really was, but at least it might not be as bad as it looked. "Can you feel your toes? Move them?" She could sense everyone's gaze on them. Zion was starting to cry. The questions hung in the air as they waited for an answer.

"Yeah," AJ finally said. But when he tried to scoot forward, he stopped with a groan. "I think I'm just stuck. But I'm really stuck."

Wyatt's voice rang out. "Okay, everybody, we've got to get that log off AJ."

"How are we going to do that?" Zion said through tears. "It's too big."

"No it's not," Wyatt insisted. "Not if we all lift together. We just need to give him an inch or two. And then AJ, you'll use your elbows to drag yourself forward."

"Sure," AJ said.

Wyatt looked at them. About half the group was on each side of the log. "Okay, guys, stay on whatever side of the trunk you're on and get on either side of AJ. I want the strongest people closest to him."

They each found a space facing the log. Natalia was across from Wyatt, both of them on the left side of AJ's body. Although she shouldn't think of that word with regards to AJ, because *body* sounded too much like something dead.

"Okay. This is what we're going to do. When I give the word, we're going to keep our heads up, push our butts back, and squat down with our backs straight. Don't let your knees get ahead of your toes. Then we'll all quickly find a knot or a branch or anything to grab on to underneath. And then we'll tighten our bellies and lift on my count. Everybody ready?"

There was a chorus of agreement.

"Okay, AJ, be ready to move as soon as you feel the log moving." Wyatt took a deep breath. "Now, everybody else, keep your back straight, bend your knees, stick your butt back, and squat."

Natalia's knees grazed the rough bark as she followed Wyatt's instructions.

"Reach under and find something to hold on to before we lift."

Her fingers found a crack, and she pressed them into it.

"Now on my count tighten your belly, straighten your knees, and lift. One. Two. Three. Go."

Natalia gritted her teeth and heaved. Or tried to. The log didn't seem to have moved at all. Her elbows pressed against her knees and her lower back protested as she strained to stand. The air was torn by grunts and shouts as they all struggled to raise the trunk. But centimeter by centimeter, it edged a tiny bit higher. The muscles in her upper arms started to quiver.

"Go, AJ, go!" Wyatt ordered.

And suddenly AJ was worming his way out. And then he was free.

"Okay, everyone get your body parts out of the way and on my count let go." Wyatt took a deep breath. "One. Two. Three. Drop!"

The trunk landed without crushing anyone's toes. In fact, it was still about four inches above the ground, supported by a broken branch farther up or just the natural contours of the land. That small space must be the reason that AJ didn't have a broken back.

To Natalia's immense relief, AJ got to his knees and then his feet. She went up to him and touched his arm. "Do you have any numbness or tingling?"

"No." He rubbed the small of his back. "I think I'm going to have one hell of a bruise, though."

"Do you mind if I look?"

For an answer, he turned around, tugging up his shirt and backpack. In the light from her headlamp, the skin was abraded, dotted with blood.

"Is it okay if I touch your spine?"

"Go ahead."

She reached under his shirt and with her fingertips pressed his spine from the curve of his back down to the crack of his buttocks. He was as furry on the back as he was on the front, but she was past feeling grossed out. AJ sucked in his breath toward the end, but otherwise didn't complain. She repeated the movements on each side. But her fingers found no lumps or unexpected edges, and AJ didn't hiss in pain.

Her shoulders loosened. "I think you're okay."

Susan gave AJ a hug. "Oh, honey, I'm so glad."

Natalia looked around the ring of faces. Her headlamp played over them one by one. She saw exhaustion, fear, and grim determination. What emotions did her own face betray?

Wyatt sighed. "I think we need to stop and rest for a while. It's too dangerous."

"Dangerous?" Jason echoed. "What about what's behind us?"

"We've put some distance between us and the fire." Marco cleared his throat and spit. "And B's phone is dead, and mine almost is, which means no more flashlights. I don't feel safe trying to keep walking in the dark." He hadn't complained once about hiking in open-toed Tevas, but Natalia figured it couldn't be easy.

"It feels like we've all used up a year's supply of adrenaline." Pushing up his worthless sunglasses, Darryl scrubbed his face with his hands. "Everyone's dead on their feet."

"And I'm hungry." Zion sounded like he was close to tears.

"I don't know." Natalia couldn't keep her voice from trembling. "Is it really safe? What if the wind picks up or changes direction?"

"I'm not saying we sleep for eight hours," Wyatt said gently. "But if we keep pushing without a break, I think we're just asking for more injuries. As soon as we come to a clearing, let's stop and eat something, check the map, and rest for an hour or two. Even if you don't sleep, it will recharge your batteries. In Eagle Scouts, we call it STOP. *Stop, Think, Observe, Plan.*"

The others nodded in agreement. Reluctantly, Natalia did, too.

## CHAPTER 18

# NAKED AND AFRAID

2:17 A.M.

**"I THINK THIS IS** as good a spot as any." Wyatt turned in a circle in the small clearing they had just reached. "It's flat and relatively clear."

People were already sitting, going through their packs or smoothing out a place to lie down. Wyatt had set down Trask, and now his parents were fussing over him. Natalia tilted her head back. It should have been a clear night, but the stars were obscured by a haze of smoke.

"Hey, guys," Wyatt said. "Before we try to rest, I think we should take inventory. Does anyone besides me have a water filter, like a LifeStraw?" When people shook their heads, he said, "I only have one, but if everyone fills up their bottles at the creek, we can pass it around and take turns using it." He knelt by his backpack, which Marco had set down, unzipped it, and found first the filter and then a tiny silver square that turned out to be an emergency blanket. He spread it out. "Why don't we put whatever we've got on here."

"I sure hope our cars are okay," Marco said as he pulled a set of keys from his pocket. "Mine's a real classic. A 1966 Sunbeam Alpine. They don't make them like that anymore."

"Marco has a thing for cars old enough to have belonged to his grandparents," Beatriz teased as she set down her towel and water bottle on the space blanket. "Cars so old that they spend more time up on lifts with him tinkering on them than they do on the road. Some days I think he loves that car more than he loves me."

Wyatt said, "I guess we don't need to add our phones or keys, not unless there's something useful on your key chain." Marco repocketed his keys.

"About all we have is a diaper," Lisa said, "which I'm going to use right now. Oh, and some hand sanitizer." She picked up Trask and carried him behind a tree.

With Trask fussing in the background, people took items from their packs and pockets and added them to the silver square. For his grandpa's benefit, Zion narrated each addition. Marco added the leash he'd been wearing around his neck. In his pockets he had a pair of sunglasses, an inhaler, and a bandanna. A few people had food: an apple, a handful of baby carrots in a plastic bag, two Nature Valley granola bars, a small bag of almonds, a KIND bar. AJ's pack had a book about easy day hikes, sunscreen, and an aerosol can that turned out to be bear spray. People looked at each other but didn't comment.

From her pack, Natalia added a LUNA bar, her whistle, her first aid kit, and her beach towel. But she found herself reluctant to pull out one item: her phone charger. A bunch of people were going to want to use it. Her phone was still at 43 percent, but the idea of it going to zero, of not being able to communicate once they were back in range of a cell tower, made her feel itchy with panic. Finally she pulled it out and added it to the pile.

"Wait—is that a phone charger?" Marco leaned forward. He was cradling Blue like a big furry baby while on one side Beatriz rubbed his belly and on the other Susan scratched behind his ears.

"My grandpa's phone is down to seven percent," Zion said.

Jason held up his. "Mine's at sixteen."

"I know it has enough to recharge one phone from zero to a hundred," Natalia said. "I don't know if that means it can get like three phones to thirty-three percent."

Wyatt said, "Let's start by having Marco hook up to it first and at least get him up to twenty so he and Beatriz can have a light source. And then we can decide who gets it next." As he spoke, he started pulling things out of his pack and pockets. He had the most of anyone. In addition to the space blanket, map, headlamp, first aid kit, parachute cord, and compass, he also had two Clif bars, two PowerBars, his and Marco's sunscreen, a knife, rain pants, a fleece jacket, a T-shirt, something in a stuff sack he called a bivy bag, and an emergency waterproof poncho that folded down to a square.

"What's that?" Beatriz pointed at a four-inch-long orange plastic tube Wyatt was adding to the pile.

"It's a whistle, but it's also got a compass, a signal mirror, and a flint fire starter. And the whole thing is a waterproof match holder."

"You should go on that TV show *Naked and Afraid*,"

Marco said. "That would be perfect for the one item you're allowed to bring on."

Next, Wyatt added a flattened roll of TP and a small trowel. Seeing them reminded Natalia about how many hours she had been ignoring her need to go. Intuiting people's thoughts, Wyatt said, "After this, I'll dig a trench behind a tree and we can take turns using it. Start at one end, cover your poop, and try not to use too much TP."

From his pants pocket, Darryl pulled out a yellow box and reluctantly added it to the pile.

"EpiPens?" Wyatt asked. "For you?"

"Zion. He's allergic to bees."

Susan's pack, which had a sleeping bag strapped to the bottom, had some duplicates of Wyatt's items. She also had a small stove, coffee-making supplies, a bandanna, a bungie cord, and something that looked like a red stick of dynamite.

"A road flare?" AJ asked. "Why do you have that?"

Susan frowned in frustration as she sought the right words. "It begins the fire camp."

Wyatt helped her out. "Some people use it as a camp-fire starter. It burns itself up so the only thing you need to pack out is the plastic cap."

"Why not just use matches?" Zion asked.

"Matches take up less space, but flares don't require kindling, and they'll even work on damp wood."

"I guess the one thing we don't need to worry about is how to start a fire," Natalia said. Still, something about the flare nagged her. Maybe she'd seen one recently, marking the site of an accident?

The last thing out of Susan's pack was a quart-sized plastic bag. Natalia's mouth watered when she saw what it was filled with: a mix of raisins, M&M's, and peanuts.

Wyatt added it to the other food. The pile looked large until Natalia thought about how it had to be split a dozen ways.

"What about you, Jason?" Ryan asked. "Don't you have anything to add to the pile?" He exchanged a meaningful glance with Lisa, who had returned with Trask. The toddler was crying, the sound rhythmic and exhausted.

Jason was wearing cargo shorts with what seemed like dozens of pockets. He shook his head. "Nope. I don't have anything."

Getting to his feet, Marco moved closer to him. "That's not true. I've seen you patting your pockets all night. What have you got in there?"

Jason stood up, too, as did AJ. Slowly, reluctantly, Jason pushed his hands into his front pockets. But when they emerged a second later, they were empty. He held them out. "Like I said, I've got nothing, dude."

As Jason spoke Blue hunched his shoulders and bared his teeth. The faintest of growls buzzed around him.

"Let me help you look." Marco crowded closer and then grabbed one of his arms, while AJ grabbed the other. Jason shouted and twisted in protest.

"I got this," Marco said. His free hand pushed into one of Jason's pockets. When he pulled it out, something glinted on his palm. People gasped in surprise. Whatever it was, it certainly wasn't food.

Wyatt got to his feet and stepped closer so that his

headlamp illuminated it. The object was a little smaller than Marco's palm. Shaped something like a snowflake, it was made of dozens of twinkling white gems. Set inside the snowflake shape was a cross made of red shimmering stones. The place where the arms of the cross met was marked with a sparkling jewel the size of a dime.

"Oh my God," Beatriz breathed. "Are those real diamonds?"

Jason opened his mouth but nothing came out. Natalia felt like she could almost hear his thoughts as they scrambled around, looking for an explanation.

Into the silence came a crashing sound behind them. It got louder by the second. The darkness seemed to amplify it. Snapping, cracking, splintering. A bolt of adrenaline shot down Natalia's spine. What could make that kind of noise?

The jewelry forgotten, they tossed glances at one another, eyes wide. Lisa hugged Trask so tight he let out a startled hiccup and abruptly stopped crying.

Staring in the direction of the racket, Blue began to bark frantically. Marco grabbed his collar as he strained forward.

A deer burst into the clearing. A buck with a huge rack of antlers. Majestic and as improbable as a dream. It leapt right over the silver space blanket, clearing it easily, and then galloped back into the trees.

They were all still mesmerized, when Jason darted to the pile. He leaned down and grabbed up the can of bear spray and the plastic bag of trail mix. Then he turned and ran.

## CHAPTER 19

# IN HER BONES

2:42 A.M.

**WYATT TOOK A STEP** as if to run after Jason.

Natalia grabbed his arm. "Just let him go."

"Oh, snap!" Zion looked delighted as he put it all together. "So that thing was real?"

Marco shook his head in disbelief. "Where would somebody get something like that?"

"What was it that he was holding?" Darryl asked. "I couldn't really see it."

"It was like this big pin covered with diamonds and rubies," Beatriz explained. "And it looked old. Like something from another century."

"Maybe it wasn't real," AJ suggested.

Natalia remembered Jason's desperate expression. "Only why would anyone take fake ornate jewelry on a hike? Plus if it was fake, Jason would have said something right away."

"We know one thing for sure." Ryan made a scoffing noise. "It can't have belonged to him. So he must have stolen it."

Lisa was still jigging Trask up and down, even though he had stopped crying. "Maybe he robbed a jewelry store."

Ryan nodded. "You could be right."

Wyatt frowned. "But what kind of store would sell something like that? It looked like it belonged in a museum."

"Hey," Darryl said. "There *is* a small museum not far from here, out in the middle of nowhere, on the other side of the Columbia. It used to be an estate, and as a museum it's kind of a hodgepodge. It's been years since I was there, but I remember they had all these things that used to belong to some queen."

"What kind of things?" Beatriz asked.

"Icons. Paintings. Gowns. This elaborately carved furniture. And the queen's jewels."

"Well, whatever that was," Natalia said, "Jason's still got it, plus the bear spray."

"Bear spray would really reach out and touch someone," Marco said. "I'm glad you didn't go after him, Wyatt."

Wyatt shrugged. "I might have been okay. It's kind of counterintuitive, but pepper spray for people is actually way stronger than the pepper spray for bears."

"I wish he hadn't taken that food," Zion said. "I'm really hungry."

Natalia looked down at the diminished pile of provisions. The red road flare caught her eye again, only this time she knew where she had seen it. Or part of it. Her stomach somersaulting, she leaned down and grabbed it up.

"Look at this!" Her voice was shaking as she held it up. "Look at the cap on it! It has a big red dot on the top."

"That's the striking surface," Wyatt said. "A flare is basically like a giant match."

Normally just the thought of a match would make her flinch, but not now. "Remember?" She pointed it at him. "The cap on this flare looks exactly like that plastic cap Jason was carrying while he passed us on his way in!"

Wyatt lifted one shoulder. "I didn't notice his hands."

More images crowded into her head. "When you were climbing up to get cell service, I saw Jason throwing the cap into the water. I was glaring at him because I thought he was littering, and he was glaring right back." Natalia exhaled sharply as it all came into focus. "But he was really getting rid of the evidence."

"Evidence of what?" Marco asked.

AJ's voice cracked with excitement as he said what Natalia was thinking. "Wyatt said people use road flares to start fires. Jason must have started the fire."

Ryan sounded skeptical. "And then he went hiking?"

But Natalia knew in her bones that was what had happened. She looked around the ring of faces. "I'm guessing something happened that Jason didn't expect. He was probably in a car accident, put out a flare, and then it accidentally caught the grass on fire." No wonder he had been in such a hurry when he passed her and Wyatt. He had been running away from the fire. The fire he had accidentally caused. "And then he kept quiet and hoped that nobody noticed."

"But you did notice," Wyatt said. "You said you glared at him when he tossed the cap into the water. So he knows you saw it."

"Oh my God, Natalia." Beatriz put her hand over her mouth. "And then he tried to push you off at Sky Bridge."

It all made sense now. "And when I was looking for Susan, I kept feeling like someone was following me. I didn't say anything because I thought I was imagining it."

Wyatt didn't say anything, just put his arms around Natalia and pulled her close.

Blue whined and nosed Darryl, who stumbled backward a half step.

Zion threw his arms around the dog's neck. "It's okay, Blue," he said, but his voice shook.

"What's he going to do?" Lisa clutched Trask tighter. "What's Jason going to do now that all of us know?"

## CHAPTER 20

# IS THIS TOO CLOSE?

2:25 A.M.

**RYAN PUT HIS UNBURNED** hand on Lisa's shoulder. "It's okay, honey. He's certainly not going to do anything tonight. He's too busy running away."

Darryl laughed without mirth. "And what could he do to us that would be worse than what's already happening?"

Zion puffed out his chest. "Plus there's ten of us and only one of him. Eleven if you count Trask."

"For now, let's not think about Jason. Stick to the original plan," Beatriz said.

Wyatt nodded. "Beatriz is right. We'll eat something, drink a little water, and try to sleep for a couple of hours."

Lisa's hand sanitizer started going from hand to hand, as Wyatt began cutting up the apple and the various bars with his knife. Without the bag of trail mix, the amount of food looked pitifully small.

"Anyone have allergies?" Wyatt asked. As people shook their heads, he arranged the results until they were more or less eleven equal piles.

Darryl said, "Zion can have my share."

Wyatt shook his head. "Zion won't starve to death, and we all need to eat a little something to keep on going."

"I'm not that hungry anyway, Grandpa," Zion said loyally.

As people gathered up their share of the food, Wyatt redistributed anything extra they could use to keep warm: beach towels, foil blankets, rain jackets, and extra clothes.

Some people ate quickly, while others tried to savor their few bites. With a whine, Blue nosed Darryl until Marco hauled the dog back and apologized for his begging. Natalia slipped Blue her bit of apple, and she wasn't the only one who shared with the dog.

"Come on, Susan, you need to eat," AJ coaxed.

Susan was sitting with her back against a tree trunk, her untouched food in a pile in her lap. She started to bring a carrot to her lips, then stopped when her headlamp illuminated her scratches. "What happened to my arms?"

"Oh, you got scratched a little bit," Darryl said. "But you're okay."

She put her fingers to her temples. "I wish I could think. Lately I feel like someone put my head in a bucket of Jell-O."

Darryl tried to make a joke of it. "Even Jell-O sounds good right about now."

Marco had carried a clutch of water bottles to the nearby stream and filled them. Now Wyatt's water filtration device went from person to person. The bottom end of the short tube went into the water, while the top of the tube was capped with a plastic straw. When it was their turn to use it, some people rubbed the end of the straw on their shirts. Natalia didn't bother.

It took more effort to suck the water up through the straw than she had thought, enough that her cheeks went hollow. Even though it wasn't much, just a few mouthfuls of food and water made her feel stronger, like a plant in the desert after a rain, its limp leaves lifting.

"You were right about us needing to stop," she said, passing the filtration device back to Wyatt. Even though it was his, he was the last to use it. "I do feel better."

"We're all dead on our feet."

With the food gone, people began to curl up and try to get comfortable. The clearing was small enough that they were all only a few feet apart. They were in pairs. Marco and Beatriz, with Blue between them and her beach towel over them. Darryl and Zion shared a space blanket. Ryan and Lisa had Trask between them and a couple of rain jackets over them. Even Susan and AJ lay next to each other, she in her sleeping bag and he underneath a space blanket. They weren't close enough for it to be called cuddling, but perhaps they still spread a little warmth to each other.

Wyatt picked up a small bag that had come from his pack. "You'll want to take off your boots before you get into the bivy bag," he told Natalia.

"It's yours, though. Are you sure you don't want to use it?"

"I'll be fine," he said. "I've got a beach towel."

Natalia unlaced her boots and pulled them off, ignoring how it made the pain on her blistered toe come into focus again. She was definitely not taking off her socks. She didn't want to know how bad it was. On the horizon, fires patched and speckled the slopes so that, in the dark, the distant hillside looked like a lava flow.

She swallowed and turned away. After toggling off her headlamp, she began to wriggle her way into the bivy bag. It was like a narrow sleeping bag, only without any padding. The outside was dark orange. The inside was the same silvery stuff as a foil blanket.

Unbidden, the memory of how her mom used to wrap Conner up like a burrito popped into her thoughts. With the memory came pain so sharp and sudden it was like someone had slipped a knife between her ribs and given it a twist. Her mom always said babies liked the security of being swaddled. But the tightness of the bag around her legs just made Natalia feel trapped.

As she rocked from side to side to pull the bag past her hips, Wyatt smoothed a space with the flat of his hands, occasionally tossing a rock into the trees ringing the clearing. He stretched out and then patted the ground in front of him. By accident or design, the way he was lying meant Natalia couldn't face the fire without also facing him. In the limited space, that would have put their faces only a few inches apart, which seemed too intimate. Besides, she was hyperaware of how long it had been since she had brushed her teeth. So she lay with her back to him, her arms outside the bag, and the fire out of her direct range of sight.

Wyatt's warm breath stirred the hairs on the nape of her neck. "Is this too close?" he whispered.

"No. It's fine." The whole length of her body was suddenly aware of his body behind her, not quite touching but not quite *not* touching, either.

The ground was unyielding. Despite Wyatt's efforts, rocks dug into Natalia's hip and shoulder and the arm she had curled under her head.

A good portion of the sky glowed red, as did the moon. The flames cast a strange yellow light that sometimes grew so bright she could see everything around them. Then the light would die down, and it would get darker again. She forced herself to close her eyes.

What if they all drifted off and awoke only when it was too late, when the trees ringing them burst into flame? She remembered reading about a forest fire that had overrun a group of smoke jumpers, firefighters who parachuted in to fight the flames. They had deployed their emergency shelters, supposedly safe to five hundred degrees—and roasted alive inside them.

Natalia's eyes flew open. What if her staying awake was the only thing keeping them all safe? Keeping them alive? She started to shiver. She tried to will it to stop but failed.

Wyatt's fingers cupped her hip. "Are you cold?" He hitched his lower body a half inch closer. Now she could feel his knees against the backs of her own.

"I'm not cold." His touch made her tremble even harder. "I don't know why I'm shaking."

"Animals shake after they escape a predator. It's your body processing everything that's happened tonight."

Closing her eyes, she twisted her head back toward Wyatt. In the lightest of whispers, she said, "I'm afraid of fire. It's personal for me." What was she doing? She never talked about what had happened.

"I guessed it might be."

"You did?"

"You told me earlier that you were afraid of fire. And when you rolled up your pants to go wading, I saw the scars on the back of your leg." Wyatt had told her to bring a swimsuit, but Natalia had pretended she had forgotten.

"Oh." She'd thought she had been careful not to expose her scars, with their thickness, their odd color. Another shiver, more violent, rocked her. Wyatt hitched himself even closer. Now she could feel his chest against her shoulder blades. "When I was in fifth grade, there was a fire. My house burned down. And my little brother died."

It was a version of the truth, told in the passive voice. Told in passing. As if it weren't Natalia's fault. As if it weren't the one thing that had shaped every day since.

"Oh, Natalia, I'm so sorry."

The darkness, and the fact she couldn't see his face, allowed her to say the next part. The worst part.

"It was all my fault. I'm the one who started the fire."

The words seemed to hang in the air.

She whispered the rest in a rush. "I tried to save him by holding him out the second-floor window. But he fell." Her breathing hitched when she exhaled. Wasn't Wyatt going to say anything?

Wyatt finally broke the silence. "Did you say you were in fifth grade?"

"Yeah."

"So just a couple of years older than Zion?"

She realized this was probably true. Even though Zion seemed so small. So young. So helpless. "Yeah." Something inside her chest felt loosened the tiniest bit.

After another long silence, Wyatt sighed and said, "It's hard not to try to take responsibility for everything, even things not in your control. Like right now. What if I've made the wrong decision about us taking a break? Then it will be my fault if it all goes south."

"No, it won't." Natalia shifted again, but it was like trying to get comfortable on concrete. The only enjoyable part was feeling his warmth behind her. "You're doing the best you can. And you know more about the outdoors than any of us."

"Just like I'm sure you did the best you could with what you knew back then. And look at what you've done tonight. You helped Ryan and AJ and Lisa."

She felt a small surge of pride but still couldn't stop arguing. "And if we all burn up, none of that will matter."

"Won't it? Everyone dies, but that doesn't mean that what happens in between being born and dying doesn't count." He sighed. "But I guess we can't solve life's mysteries tonight. You should at least try to get a few minutes' sleep."

"Okay." Obediently Natalia again closed her eyes, but

sleep wouldn't come. Lisa and Ryan were talking in low voices. Marco's cough had become constant. Then Darryl began to snore, the sound a cross between a grumble and a chain saw. Her back felt stiff. Even the novelty of having Wyatt so close wore off. At one point she started to doze, but as her body relaxed another rock jabbed her. She jerked awake again.

The dark, empty minutes crawled by. How long the night was, and how slowly it passed. She imagined saying that to Dr. Paris. But wouldn't Dr. Paris point out that no matter how long it felt, it was always finite?

Suddenly Beatriz shrieked. Those who had been sleeping startled awake. To her surprise, Natalia realized she might have been one of them.

Wyatt and a few others were on their feet, their hands balled into fists as if ready to fight. Natalia pushed herself to her knees, the bivy sack tight around her lower body.

"What's wrong, B?" Marco's voice was filled with alarm.

"Sorry! Sorry! Something just crawled over my arm."

Before anyone could respond, a crash came from the woods behind them.

Susan gasped. "What was that?"

"Is it Jason?" Lisa clutched Trask, who let out a startled hiccup.

From the woods came a strange noise that reminded Natalia of Chewbacca from Star Wars. A howl, wordless but filled with emotion.

Snorting and snuffling, three dark creatures lumbered

into the edge of the clearing. One huge. Two smaller. A mother bear and her cubs.

Natalia let out an involuntary shriek. The mother's heavy head swung around. And suddenly Natalia was transported back to her nightmares.

## CHAPTER 21

# TRY NOT TO THINK ABOUT IT

## SIX YEARS EARLIER

"NO, NO, NO!" THE dark beast leapt toward Natalia, jaws spread wide. She cowered, wrapping her arms around her head. Knowing it wouldn't make any difference.

"Natalia! Wake up! Natalia!"

The beast shook her back and forth. Its teeth sank into her upper arms.

"Natalia! Honey!" Not an animal's growl but her mom's voice. "Wake up! You're just having another nightmare. You're all right."

Natalia opened her eyes. The pressure on her arms wasn't from teeth but her mom's frantic fingers. It was night. She and her parents were standing in the parking lot of their new apartment building. Against the icy blacktop, her feet were bare. She was dressed only in thin pajamas, but that wasn't why she was shivering, vibrating so hard it felt like she might fly apart. In her dream, a great dark beast had been chasing her.

During the day, the fire was never far from her thoughts. She often imagined the smell of smoke or thought she caught the flicker of flames with the corner of an eye. But at night, she drowned, or dangled from cliffs, or was crushed in car accidents, or fought off monsters both human and animal. Natalia didn't know if it was a blessing that she never dreamed of the fire.

Now her mom held her upper arms, while her dad stood watching, his big hands empty, dangling helplessly. Both their faces were drawn with guilt and grief. In the building behind them, lights were coming on and curtains pushed back as their new neighbors gawped or silently cursed at them. This wasn't the first time Natalia had woken up outside screaming. With no memory of how she had gotten there. Of how she must have undone the two locks and the chain on their new front door.

When she'd finally come home from the hospital, it wasn't home at all. It was this anonymous apartment building, while their house was being rebuilt. Only a few things hadn't been ruined by the smoke, flames, or the water from the firefighters' hoses: a teapot, a few utensils, a couple of cast-iron frying pans. That was it. But it was petty to miss her favorite clothes and books. Not when her brother was dead.

"That's it," her dad said. "This can't go on. She has to see someone."

"N-no." It was an effort for Natalia to speak. Her head still felt muddled. When her mom finally let go of her arms, she half expected to feel hot blood dripping off her elbows. "I don't want to talk to anyone. I just want to be left alone."

"You're not getting any better, Natalia." Her dad sighed heavily. "I'm afraid you don't have a choice."

~

"I'm Dr. Paris," the psychiatrist said. She had just firmly told Natalia's mom it would be best for them to talk alone. Now she put out her hand. Hesitantly, Natalia took it. She had never shaken a grown-up's hand before, and she knew immediately she was doing it wrong. Her grip was too weak, too wishy-washy. It was surely being judged and found wanting.

Dr. Paris's expression didn't betray her thoughts. She was tall, probably as tall as Natalia's father. Her thick dark blond hair was pulled back into a messy bun. Her eyes were the color of faded denim. Her gray turtleneck was topped with a scarf in shades of blue and green.

She looked nothing like Natalia's petite, dark-haired mother. Her mother, who was out in the waiting room, probably anxiously twisting her hands. Her mother, who couldn't help her. No one could.

"Why don't we both sit down," Dr. Paris said, taking her own suggestion as Natalia sat in a matching dark leather chair. "Do you know why you're here, Natalia?"

"My parents made me come. Because I don't really sleep anymore."

"If they hadn't made you, would you have come on your own?"

"No." She surprised herself by being honest. "I just want to be left alone."

"Is there anything else your parents are concerned about besides you not sleeping?"

"I'm not doing that great in school." Natalia was always on the lookout for danger. It was more than just checking and rechecking to make sure the stove was off at home. When her mom drove her to school, she watched oncoming cars, sure they would swerve into their lane. At school, the sudden slam of a door would become a gun shot.

Dr. Paris's face remained calm. "And why do you think you're having these experiences?"

Natalia gritted her teeth, suddenly angry. The anger swelling her veins felt good. It made her feel powerful. No longer lost and afraid. "My mom must have told you what happened. You must know."

"Why don't you explain it to me?"

"My little brother died in a fire four months ago. Conner died, and it was all my fault."

"Why was it your fault?"

"Because I did everything wrong. I'm the one who started the fire. I'm the one who couldn't put it out. I'm the one who tried to hold him out the window. And I'm the one who dropped him and broke his neck." Most days Natalia felt like she had really died that day, too. That she was dead and no one else knew it yet.

Her breathing had sped up. Her muscles were tight. Thinking about Conner made her feel like her heart was going to explode.

"Natalia!" Dr. Paris said.

Natalia was vaguely aware it wasn't the first time the psychiatrist had said her name.

"Natalia, I need you to tell me five things you can see, four things you can touch, three things you can hear, two things you can smell, and one thing you can taste."

"What?" She was sinking deeper into herself and could barely hear her.

"Tell me five things you can see. Right now. Go!"

"Um." Natalia refocused. "My hands, a box of Kleenex, your scarf, the blinds, and um, that photo of a flower."

"Good. Now named four things you could touch."

"Okay." Natalia tried to find new things to mention. "My jeans, the wooden arm of this chair, the coffee table, that silver paperweight on your desk." Each answer took her out of herself just a little bit more. And by the time she was down to one thing she could taste—she picked the blue pack of Trident lying on the desktop—her heart and breathing were almost back to normal.

"You might already know this," Dr. Paris said, "but what you just experienced was a panic attack. Panic attacks, anxiety, insomnia, flashbacks—those are all classic signs of PTSD. Post-traumatic stress disorder. I believe that's what you have."

"Doesn't that just happen to soldiers?"

"No. It can happen to anyone who has been through a trauma. Your nervous system has gotten stuck in overdrive. So your muscles are always tense, your breathing is always sped up. Your nervous system is trying to prepare you for an emergency that isn't actually happening. We can unstick it. But to do that we're going to look at what happened that day."

Natalia was already shaking her head. "I try not to think about it. Not ever."

Dr. Paris tilted her head. "Does it work?"

A silence hung in the air before she finally admitted the truth. "No."

"A lot of people with PTSD think they'll be fine if they just don't think about it. So they put what happened in a suitcase and then put the suitcase high on a shelf and close the door. But the reality is it still comes back. And back. And back. That's why you're having nightmares and sleepwalking. But if we take what happened out of the suitcase and look at it, then we'll be able to pack it up and really put it away. If you just shove it in the suitcase, you can't really close it."

"I just want to go back to normal." Her voice broke.

"I've got some bad news, which is also good news. Do you know what caterpillars do in a cocoon?"

Natalia resisted the sudden urge to roll her eyes. She could feel the cliché coming. "They grow wings."

"No. They dissolve."

She blinked. "What?"

"They become completely liquid. Then the cells reconfigure themselves into something totally different. Into a butterfly."

Natalia absorbed this. She couldn't decide if it was gross or cool. Maybe both.

"Trauma does the same thing. So if you're hoping you'll be like you were before, you'll wait forever. You're going to become something completely different."

# CHAPTER 22

# DON'T PLAY DEAD

4:01 A.M.

**WYATT GOT TO HIS** feet in one fluid motion. Standing tall, Wyatt looked the mama bear directly in the eye. In a strong, firm voice, he said, "Get out of here, bear!"

Marco clamped his hand around Blue's snout. Darryl pushed Zion behind his back.

In a softer voice, Wyatt warned them, "No screaming. No sudden movements. And whatever you do, don't run." His eyes never wavered from the mama bear. "Slowly stretch out your arms to make yourself look as big as possible. If you're wearing a coat, unzip it and hold it open." Out of the corner of her left eye, Natalia could see him following his own advice as he spoke. "Bears normally stay away from humans, but there's the fire, and she's got her cubs."

Time stretched like taffy while the bears and the humans stared at each other. The three animals were the color of midnight, the only lighter patches of fur around their snouts. Natalia's heart hammered in her ears as she fixed her gaze on the mother bear. The bear's eyes were as big as chestnuts, gleaming in the pulsing radiance from the fire.

On her knees in the bivy bag, Natalia suddenly felt dizzy. She swayed involuntarily.

The mama bear made a woofing noise. Saliva glistened on her big, white teeth. She snapped her jaws, biting the air. Her cubs shifted anxiously back and forth.

"She's going to charge!" AJ's voice shook.

"I don't think so." Wyatt slowly moved behind Natalia. He stepped over her bent legs until he had one foot on either side. His knees pressed into her shoulder blades, steadying her, keeping her from falling over. "She doesn't want a fight any more than we do. She's just afraid and trying to intimidate us." He raised his voice. "Go away, bear! Go away!"

For an answer, the mama bear growled and laid her ears back. Blowing and snorting, she swatted the ground with one front paw.

"Calm down!" Wyatt ordered. "We're not going to hurt you or your cubs." In a softer voice, he said, "If she does attack, whatever you do, don't play dead. Try to hit and kick her in the face and muzzle."

Suddenly, the bear started to gallop toward Natalia.

Now there were only a dozen feet between them. Natalia's heart seized in her chest. Her legs were still bound up by the bivy bag. This was going to end the way her dreams always did, with blood and terror.

Seven feet.

"No!" Natalia shouted. "No! Go away!"

Wyatt's commands joined hers. Then somehow, with his strong arms assisting her, she was on her feet.

Three feet.

The bear was close enough that Natalia could smell her, a sweet musky smell. Soon those heavy jaws would close on her flesh. This was it, then.

But at the last second, the mama bear pivoted on one huge paw, turned, and ran back toward her cubs. Bumping and shouldering them ahead of her, she pushed them back into the trees, away from both the fire and the people.

And then all three bears were gone, as if they had never been. As if they had just been another of Natalia's bad dreams. Over the years, the nightmares had lessened, but never completely left her.

For a long moment no one stirred. Then everyone began to talk at once, exclaiming and even laughing nervously in relief.

AJ exhaled noisily. "That was close!"

"She was trying to bluff us," Wyatt said. "Trying to make sure we stayed well back before she took off." At some point he had wrapped his arms around Natalia, and now he gave her a long squeeze. His soft lips touched the back of her neck, and for a few seconds she forgot everything else. Then he let her go. He started pushing down the bivy bag so she could get out.

Lisa was shaking her head. "Maybe it's actually a good thing we don't have any food."

"And that the bears didn't think I smelled like barbecue," Ryan added.

Darryl scrubbed his face with his hands. "The only thing we probably smell like is sweat."

"Were those grizzly bears?" Zion asked, wide-eyed.

"Black bears," Wyatt said. "And black bears are mostly scared of you." He turned, to Marco. "Good thing you managed to keep Blue quiet."

"And that he's such a good dog," Susan crooned, moving closer to scratch behind his ears.

Feeling stiff and sour-mouthed, Natalia finished freeing her legs from the bivy sack. On the outside, the sack was slick with dew, the way her skin was now covered with a fine sheen of sweat.

"Well, I guess we're all wide-awake now," Wyatt said. "Might as well get ready and get back on the trail."

The sun hadn't yet broken over the horizon, but it was light enough for Natalia to notice the exhaustion etched on people's faces. And to see tatters of smoke eddying through the tree trunks.

Ignoring the pain of the popped blister, Natalia thrust her feet into her boots. After tying her laces, she pulled on her headlamp and switched it on. Scratching a mosquito bite on her arm, she checked to make sure no one else was using the trench Wyatt had dug behind a tree before making for it.

When she came back, people were shoving feet into boots and pushing things back into packs and pockets. With Trask already on his back, Wyatt was looking at the map, illuminated by his headlamp.

"Where are we exactly?" She stifled a groan as she shouldered her own pack.

He pointed, then traced a route with his finger. "We're going to have to cross a creek here, then we'll gain some elevation, drop back down again, and then skirt this little lake. After that, it's only another three miles or so until we hit a road.

Natalia picked out Basin Falls on the map. It didn't look like they had come very far. "Are we even halfway there?"

"Maybe a little more."

That didn't seem like nearly enough. Everyone was hungry and tired. Tired to the bone.

Trask was fussing, arching backward, his face creased into an angry frown. He must be hungry as well as tired. Fishing in her pocket, Natalia found the chunk of KIND bar she'd saved. She held it out to Lisa. "Is it okay if I give Trask this?"

Lisa put her hand on her heart. "That would be really nice of you. Thank you."

As Trask reached for it with his chubby hand, Natalia thought of Conner. For the first time, the memory of her little brother wasn't as sharp as a blade.

"We need to start moving," Wyatt said. "The wind is picking up."

He was right. She felt the wind push her hair back from her face.

Which meant it was pushing the fire straight toward them.

## CHAPTER 23

# LIKE A ZOMBIE

### 4:33 A.M.

**THEY SET OFF AGAIN.** Wyatt led the way, occasionally pulling the map and compass from his pockets. At first the trail was thin, just a faint scuffed line winding among the trees. Would they even have been able to keep to it in the dark?

"Where do you think Jason is?" Natalia asked Wyatt after they had been hiking for about forty-five minutes. They had seen no sign of him. It felt like they were alone in the world—just them, the trees, and the fire trying to catch up to them.

"Are you worried he's going to do something to us?" Wyatt asked. He reached out and squeezed her hand. She still felt the tingle of his touch after his fingers fell away. "I'm guessing he's probably just trying to hightail it out of here."

The trail, wider now, ran parallel to a creek, bordered by pink, white, and yellow wildflowers. The sun hadn't yet lifted above the trees, but it was already warm.

Natalia lifted her hair off her nape. "That breeze feels good."

Wyatt's mouth twisted. "I wish it were in our faces, blowing the fire away from us."

"It's great to be able to actually see again," Darryl said from behind them. "And I'm sure Zion's glad he no longer has to be my Seeing Eye dog." Blue whined and then butted Darryl with his head. He pushed the dog's nose away. "Sorry, boy, I shouldn't have said *dog*. And I swear I don't have any food." He looked at the rest of them. "I mean, none of us do, but I'm the one he won't leave alone."

"Maybe he smells crumbs or something," AJ said. "Don't dogs have a really good sense of smell, like five hundred times better than a human's?"

Darryl shrugged. "I did have a granola bar in my pocket yesterday. But dogs don't like granola bars, do they?"

"Maybe if they get hungry enough they do. Sorry he's bugging you so much." Marco's voice was hoarse from coughing. "And, Blue, I promise I'll buy a steak when we get back to civilization."

"Poor guy," Susan said. "Poor doggy." She knuckled the top of his head.

Zion appeared at Natalia's side. "Here!" He thrust a fistful of wildflowers at her.

She was surprised. "Oh, are these for me?"

He nodded, not meeting her eyes. "For helping us."

She took them. The stems were crushed, the heads drooping. "Why, thank you."

Earlier, Wyatt had pointed out that Natalia hadn't been much older than Zion when the fire happened. Now she did the math another way. Conner had died six years ago. If he had lived, he would have been about Zion's age.

The trail turned to intersect with the creek. Wyatt checked his map. "This is where we cross."

The creek was less than a dozen feet wide and looked about a foot deep. A log served as a makeshift bridge, albeit a rounded bridge coated in velvety green moss.

Wyatt said, "If you don't think you can keep your balance up there, I would suggest just taking off your boots and wading across."

Beatriz lifted her duct-taped foot. "It's not like I can."

"Then just be careful going across. I don't think I have enough duct tape to build you a new pair."

"I know the trick," Susan said. "Look at the log. Not the water."

Beatriz began to pick her way across with Marco right behind her, hands hovering ready to catch her. Natalia helped both Ryan and Lisa take off their boots, then took off hers as well. Meanwhile, Darryl was taking off his own boots and Zion's. Blue had already drunk his fill and then splashed over to the other side. Now he was barking as if urging them all to hurry.

When Natalia pulled off her sock, it stuck to the blister. It was worse than popped. Her stupid boot had basically worn a bloody hole in her toe.

When she stepped in, she gasped at the shock of the cold water. Rocks, some slick with algae, pressed into the soles of her feet. On the other side, people were refilling their water bottles and passing around Wyatt's filter as well as the sunscreen. Marco wet his bandanna and then wrapped it around his forehead.

Wyatt was the last one over, walking across the log as easily as if it were earth. As he jumped off, he glanced down at her feet, then winced and looked closer. "That looks bad. Why didn't you put anything on it last night?"

"I didn't want to waste supplies."

"It's not wasting if you need them. Here, I've got some moleskin in my pack." After retrieving his first aid kit from Marco, Wyatt used her scissors to cut out a little doughnut shape, peeled off the backing, and then pasted it so the raw spot was now surrounded by a ring of cushioning. As she was pulling on her socks he said, "I think we need to get going." He sniffed the air again, like an animal scenting for predators. "Because the fire smells closer."

If she paid attention, she could smell it, too. Pitch and balsam, campfire and char.

Setting out again, they managed to pick up a little speed. The fire itself was harrying them forward. Not only was the air smokier, but they could hear the grumble of the flames growing louder behind them, with the occasional loud crack as a branch or even a tree fell.

Glowing orange embers began to float past them. No one said anything, just walked faster, fast enough that people sometimes tripped on a root or slid as pebbles skittered under their boots. With the help of the trekking pole, Lisa was limping along as fast as she could, but her teeth were sunk into her lip. And even though it was now full daylight, Darryl still occasionally stumbled.

Despite their increased speed, torn rags of bark laced with fire began to blow past them. Then an ember, still alight, landed a few feet from them and flared to life.

Natalia's breath caught in her chest.

Marco was on the tiny blaze in an instant, stamping it into oblivion. He upended the rest of his water bottle on the spot.

"My hero!" Beatriz clapped her hands together.

But then it happened again. Ten feet away, a burning tatter landed on a bed of needles. A puff of wind ignited the pile into a fire as big as a dinner plate. Coughing in the smoke, Marco stamped this one out too.

"Look, man," Wyatt said. "There's too many of them for us to put out. We need to concentrate on getting the heck out of here."

In silence, they hurried on. Slowly, slowly, the number of falling sparks dwindled, but the rolling smoke still stung their eyes and burned their throats. Sweat traced Natalia's spine.

From behind them, Beatriz let out a shout. "You guys, we have to stop!" Her voice was panicked.

"What's wrong?" Wyatt said.

"It's Marco."

When Natalia turned, Marco was bracing his hands on his knees. His breathing was fast and rough. The cords in his neck stood out like wires.

"He sounds like a zombie." Zion backed away.

But zombies were brain-dead and Marco looked desperate.

"It's an asthma attack," Beatriz said. "And his inhaler ran out last night."

## CHAPTER 24

# BLUE TO THE SKY

## 5:57 A.M.

SCARVES OF SMOKE AND the occasional spark were still drift-
ing past them. They couldn't afford to stop—but it was
clear Marco couldn't go on.

His eyes were panicked, his hands pressed against
his chest. As he strained to breathe, he made horrible
whistling, wheezing sounds. Every time he attempted to
inhale, his shoulders rose and a hollow triangle appeared
on each side of his neck. The muscles in his upper body
were trying—and failing—to help inflate his lungs.

Two years ago, a girl in Natalia's PE class had had an
asthma attack while they were running laps. Natalia had
experienced a visceral reaction to the idea of not being
able to breathe. She knew the consuming panic of your
body screaming for oxygen. Afterward, she had looked up
how asthma worked.

Right now, Marco's inflamed breathing tubes were
starting to squeeze shut and fill with mucus. Not only
was fresh air not getting in, but old air was trapped in his
lungs.

She stood in front of him. "Marco. Look at me. I
need you to stay calm." She put her hands on his hunched

shoulders. His shirt was soaked with sweat and he was breathing at least twice as fast as she was. "Try to relax your upper body. You need to slow your breathing down. The faster you breathe, the worse it's going to get."

Beatriz stepped closer. She had her fingers hooked in Blue's collar. Both of them were watching Natalia as if she actually knew how to fix things.

"He just got diagnosed with asthma last year," Beatriz said. "It started when he exercised—his chest would feel tight. Now other things sometimes set it off. But he doesn't really believe he has actual serious asthma."

Marco rolled his eyes at Beatriz, but she just shrugged. "What? You don't!"

Exercise could be a trigger. Marco had been hiking all night. Another trigger was allergies or irritants. Like smoke from a forest fire. Her own nose and throat felt chafed.

Untreated, asthma could kill. Marco needed to rest quietly in a room with clean air. He probably needed supplemental oxygen. But at the very minimum, he needed an inhaler, which would open up his airway to help him breathe more easily.

Natalia looked at the ring of faces surrounding them. "Does anyone else have an inhaler?"

But she already knew the answer. Marco's had been the only inhaler when they pooled all their stuff on Wyatt's blanket.

Marco cleared his throat and swallowed. "It hurts." He put one hand on his chest. "Like something pulling inside." His words were separated by gasps.

"Shh! Don't talk." Natalia put her finger to her lips. "Save your breath."

But that was actually part of the problem. He was saving his breath. Or his body was. In order to pull fresh air into his lungs, he needed to be able to push the old air out.

Natalia combined logic with what she had learned in the hospital recovering from smoke inhalation. "Try to breathe in through your nose. It will moisten the air and filter out some of the smoke. And then breathe out through your mouth. Purse your lips like you're going to whistle. Try to exhale twice as long as you inhale. That will help empty out your lungs."

As Marco followed her instructions, he started to look a little less agitated.

But as she was watching his mouth, his lips begin to slowly lose color until they were pale violet. He still wasn't getting enough oxygen.

In her head, Natalia ran through the contents of her first aid kit. Aspirin, Tylenol, Advil. Could the Benadryl help? Maybe a little, but it would also make him sleepy.

Then she thought of Zion's EpiPen, meant to reverse anaphylactic shock. In anaphylactic shock, two things happened. Blood pressure dropped as small blood vessels started to leak blood into the tissues. That wasn't Marco's problem. But anaphylactic shock also caused airways to narrow, which was exactly what was happening to Marco. Epinephrine—another word for adrenaline, the medicine in an EpiPen—narrowed blood vessels and opened airways, preparing the body for fight or flight.

Should she take Darryl aside, ask him privately? But

there wasn't time. Plus, it would be harder for him to say no in front of everyone.

"Darryl, I need to use one of Zion's EpiPens. That's the only thing we have that could help Marco."

"What? No." Darryl took a half step back. "We need to keep them for Zion."

Blue, sensing the tension, let out a sharp bark.

"Come on, man," AJ urged. "Just look at him."

Every time Marco inhaled, the notch above his collarbone sucked in a half inch.

"And you have a two-pack," Natalia pointed out. "Let me just use one. Please."

"There's two in there because the doctor said sometimes it takes two." Darryl protectively put his hand over his pocket.

"Look." Wyatt kept his voice low. "Marco could die if we don't do something right now. It won't be that long until we get back to civilization where you can get a new EpiPen. But Marco might not make it, not unless we do something now."

Darryl sighed, reached into his pocket, pulled out the box, and handed it to Natalia.

Inside were two tubes. She pulled one out and flipped back the cap, remembering the instructions they had learned in first aid class, working with a dummy injector. "Blue to the sky, orange to the thigh." The fake injector had lacked a needle, but the instructor had said the real one was strong enough to pierce even denim. Just to be sure, she raised the injector high and swung it down hard, popping it against Marco's outer thigh.

He didn't make a sound, but his eyes widened.

"One one-thousand, two one-thousand," she counted out loud. When she reached ten, she pulled the injector away. The needle automatically retracted. Starting a new count, she began to rub the spot, encouraging the medication to spread. Again, she stopped when she reached ten.

Was Marco breathing any easier? He had managed to calm himself, so his breathing was slower, but it still seemed to be requiring all his effort. Wasn't the medication supposed to work nearly instantaneously?

As she was sliding the used EpiPen back in the box next to its twin, she noticed the words on the packaging. "EpiPen Junior." What did that mean? For the thousandth time since they lost cell service, Natalia wished she could google something. Even without Google, it didn't seem good. The junior version of the EpiPen must be a smaller dose calibrated for a smaller person.

But Marco was a grown man, easily twice as heavy as Zion. Natalia muttered a swear word.

"What's the matter?" Lisa asked.

"I don't think it's enough. This says EpiPen Junior. That means it's for someone Zion's size. For an adult dose, I think I need to use both."

As if to underline her point, Marco made his loudest wheeze yet as he struggled to breathe.

Darryl shook his head. "If you use both, then we won't have anything at all."

"Come on, Grandpa!" Zion pushed his way in between them. "Marco is going to die if she doesn't!"

Looking at Marco struggling so hard to breathe, Natalia was afraid Zion was right.

"No, he isn't." Anger as well as uncertainty colored Darryl's voice. "And we have to save one for you. Just in case."

But Zion took the decision out of Darryl's hands. Grabbing the remaining injector from the open box, he pulled off the cap and in one swift motion plunged the needle into Marco's thigh.

## CHAPTER 25

# PURE TERROR

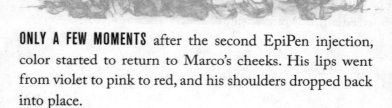

**ONLY A FEW MOMENTS** after the second EpiPen injection, color started to return to Marco's cheeks. His lips went from violet to pink to red, and his shoulders dropped back into place.

Taking a full breath, he let it out with a sigh of relief. It was echoed by everyone around him. Even Blue relaxed. He sat back on his haunches, his tongue unfurling like a pink streamer. Susan rubbed his ears.

"Thank you, man," Marco told Zion in a still-raspy voice. "I think you just saved my life." He held up his hand for a high five. Grinning proudly, Zion jumped up to slap it.

"Hey, Marco, maybe you should pull your bandanna down over your nose and mouth," AJ suggested. "It might screen out some of the smoke."

As he did, Wyatt said, "Someone besides Marco should carry my pack. We don't want his lungs working any harder than they have to."

Beatriz, Darryl, and Zion were the only ones without injuries or existing packs. "I'll do it." Beatriz slipped the straps over her shoulders, letting out a muffled groan as she hoisted it into place. She was so petite that Wyatt's pack looked oversized in comparison.

"Thanks, B," Marco said from behind his bandanna.

"Now you look like a bank robber," Zion crowed.

"Better that than a zombie." Marco's laugh turned into a cough. Natalia braced herself for the cycle to start again, but he just cleared his throat, pulled the cloth away from his face, and spit.

They started off again. The trail emerged from the trees and then cut down a seemingly endless steep, rocky slope dotted with small plants. At least the trail was mostly clear. Her stomach grumbled loud enough that at one point Wyatt looked over with a half smile. The few handfuls of food she had eaten in the middle of the night felt like they had been consumed in another decade, another life. Now she was left with a growling stomach and a headache that felt like her brain had been replaced with a stone.

Natalia let herself imagine she was back at the Dairy Barn, visualizing it as clearly as if she were really standing in front of the counter, a cold metal scoop in her right hand. What would she have? Double Chocolate Cookie Dough? Or Oh Nuts topped with hot fudge and even more nuts? A banana split? She could practically smell the sweet perfume of the banana, taste the rich ice cream melting on her tongue. The fantasy lasted to the end of the scree slope. The trail flattened out, and there were plants and bushes on either side of the trail again. Susan was in the lead, occasionally waving her single trekking pole to break the spiderwebs that stretched across.

Wyatt's voice interrupted her musings. "How are you holding up?"

"Same as everyone else. Hungry, tired, sore. At least I haven't hurt myself except for that blister." As Natalia spoke, she caught her toe and stumbled. "I guess I should be careful or I'll jinx myself."

"What about other than physically? It can't be easy, being around fire again."

"It turns out it's hard to maintain a state of pure terror for hours and hours." Now the scarves of smoke eddying past them or the occasional spark flying overhead had become the new normal. "Plus my counselor taught me that if you pay attention to physical sensations it's hard to get stuck in your own head. Because inside your head is almost always worse than reality."

"So that's how you knew what to do when AJ was freaking out?"

"Yup. Dr. Paris taught me a few tricks." She smiled at him. "But without you, we wouldn't be anyplace. You're the only one of us with a map, and maybe the only one who really knows how to read it."

Wyatt nodded. "When this fire started, we were just a group of strangers. But now we're pulling together. It's not just me or you, not anymore. It's all of us."

Natalia was opening her mouth to answer when from behind them came a shout.

"Something's wrong with Grandpa!"

<br/>

## CHAPTER 26

# NOT NEARLY ENOUGH

### 6:52 A.M.

**NATALIA WHIRLED AROUND. SEEMINGLY** oblivious to Zion's shout, Darryl kept walking unsteadily forward, his eyes at half-mast.

He almost looked like he was drunk, but that was impossible. Wasn't it?

What now? Everyone was looking at Natalia as if she could keep working magic. But what if she was fresh out of tricks?

She hurried back to Darryl. Only when she was standing nearly nose to nose with him did he stop shuffling forward.

"Out of my way!" he said irritably. "We need to keep moving."

His words sounded slurred. Had he had a stroke? But when she examined his face, it looked symmetrical, without an eye or a corner of the mouth drooping.

"This will only take a second. Can you hold out your arms for me?" She demonstrated holding her arms straight in front of her. Zion looked terrified. In an effort to lighten the atmosphere, Natalia added, "Like a zombie?"

"Why?" Darryl sounded annoyed but still complied.

He held both arms out at shoulder level, and neither one drifted down.

"And smile for me?"

It was more a grimace, a baring of the teeth, but it, too, was even. So it probably wasn't a stroke. But something was definitely wrong. Darryl looked paler, and beads of sweat dotted his forehead.

Blue whined and nosed him again. All this morning, Blue had been bothering only Darryl. No one else. While he had responded to Susan's attentions, for the last few hours he had ignored her.

Because of their keen sense of smell, dogs could detect things far earlier than humans could. Maybe Blue hadn't been sniffing for food. Hadn't Natalia read about dogs who could smell health problems like cancer or an oncoming seizure?

"Darryl?"

His eyes closed completely as his head nodded forward. He looked like he was going to sleep. Standing up.

Repeating his name, she shook his shoulders until his rheumy eyes slowly, reluctantly opened. "Darryl, are you on any medication?" As old as he was, the answer had to be yes.

He roused himself with obvious effort. "I've got a whole medicine cabinet full."

"For what?"

He made a scoffing noise. "Cholesterol. Blood pressure. Enlarged prostate." And then came the words she had already begun to suspect. "And diabetes. Type two."

Usually with a type 2 diabetic you worried about high

blood sugar. Because they were less responsive to insulin, glucose from their food could build up in their bloodstream, reaching dangerously high levels.

But just like a diabetic's blood sugar could overreact and skyrocket, it was also easy for it to plummet. And in the last twelve hours, Darryl hadn't eaten more than a couple of mouthfuls of food.

Missing meals, hiking for hours—it was only logical he had low blood sugar. By this point, all of them were probably a little hypoglycemic. But because Darryl's body did a bad job of regulating the level of sugar in his blood, he was being affected much worse than any of them. That change in his blood sugar must be what Blue had been smelling.

If he was in a full-on crisis, Darryl's breath should smell sweet even to a human nose. But when Natalia leaned forward and sniffed, all she smelled was sweat.

He swore and took a step back. "What are you doing?"

She didn't answer. She remembered the first aid instructor's words: "Blood sugar's like building a campfire. You start with kindling, small stuff that burns fast and hot, but then you need the big logs. Simple sugar is the kindling. For the big logs, you need something more complex, like trail mix."

"Does anyone have any juice or pop?" Natalia asked the group. "Hard candy? Even a cough drop? We need to get some sugar into Darryl as fast as possible."

But when she looked around, everyone was shaking their heads. Zion's eyes were wide and his hands were pressed against his mouth.

"Wait a minute!" AJ said excitedly. "Susan—didn't you have some sugar with your coffee supplies?"

At first Susan looked confused, but then her expression cleared. "Yes!" She set down her pack and fished out a plastic bag. Inside it were two sandwich bags. One was filled with coffee grounds. The other held about a quarter cup of white sugar.

Natalia tore a hole in one corner of the bag so it would act like a spout and funneled the sugar into her water bottle. Then she remembered. This was creek water, not pure water.

"Would the LifeStraw take out the sugar?" she asked Wyatt.

He bit his lip as he thought. "Yeah. I think it would. But it's better to risk him getting giardia than a diabetic coma."

She shook her water bottle hard and then handed it to Darryl. "Drink this. It'll bring your blood sugar back up."

As he tilted his head back, she wondered how long the sugar would fuel him. A few minutes? Even as long as an hour? However long it was, she was afraid it wouldn't be enough.

"I hate to say it, but don't we need to get going?" Beatriz asked. "The smoke is getting thicker." Now that they were at the bottom of the long, steep slope, they could no longer see the flames, just smoke.

Darryl handed the empty bottle back to her. "Just let me lie down for a little while."

"I'm afraid we can't," Natalia said.

Beatriz was right. The smoke was thicker.

In a panicked voice, AJ called out, "Wait a minute—where did Susan go?"

"Not again," Ryan groaned.

"There she is!" Zion pointed.

Susan pushed her way through the bushes on one side of the trail. Her hat was no longer on her head. Instead, she was holding it with red-stained hands. And inside the hat were . . .

"Blueberries!" Zion shouted.

"No, um, they're buckle . . . buckle harries."

Wyatt helped her out. "Huckleberries."

"Right!" Susan looked relieved. She held out the hat to Darryl, who put a few berries in his mouth with a trembling hand.

Natalia's elation was over almost before it began. How much time would the huckleberries actually buy? Berries were certainly better than sugar water, but they still were mostly fruit sugar, which would break down quickly. Huckleberries weren't the fuel Darryl needed to keep his internal fires burning. And once those fires were reduced to coals and ash, he really would have to lie down, because he wouldn't be able to walk. Which would be followed by seizures, coma, and finally death.

"Are you guys sure you don't have any kind of food left?" she pleaded. "Something you might have forgotten or were saving for later?"

Lisa cleared her throat. Ryan put his unburned hand on her shoulder as if to caution her, but she shook it off. "Actually, there's an Uncrustables in Trask's pack."

"What's that?" Natalia couldn't even be mad. If Trask

were her kid she might have "forgotten" about food for him, too.

"It's like a small kid's sandwich with peanut butter and jelly. They call it that because they cut off the crusts."

The jelly would only provide Darryl with additional sugar. The bread would be a slightly more complex carbohydrate. But the peanut butter would be the big log. Its protein and fat could give Darryl the endurance he needed.

Wyatt turned his back to Lisa to give her access to the child carrier. Trying not to wake Trask, she gingerly unzipped the pocket holding the wrapped sandwich. Meanwhile, Susan showed the others what to look for, and they began to search for more huckleberries.

The smoke had thickened, and now it rolled down the hill toward them like fog. They were all coughing now, but at least Marco wasn't coughing any more than anyone else.

Lisa ripped open the packaging and handed the sandwich to Darryl. It was no bigger than the palm of his hand. But Natalia thought it might be just enough.

It was going to have to be.

While Darryl chewed and swallowed, Beatriz came up to Natalia with cupped hands and red-stained lips. "Here, try some."

Natalia popped a berry between her lips. She let it rest on her tongue for a second, dusty and warm. Then she pressed it against the roof of her mouth until it exploded on her tongue, sweet and sour and a little grainy. Saliva flooded her mouth. Meanwhile the others were popping berries in their mouths as quickly as they were plucked.

Darryl was already looking better. They were going to make it. Her shoulders relaxed.

Wyatt and Ryan were bent over the map while Wyatt traced a path with his finger.

"So you think three hours tops?" Ryan asked.

"Um, guys . . . ," AJ said in a shaky voice. At his tone, Natalia's heart jolted in her chest. She turned and looked up.

The fire had reached the top of the ridge above them. Flames leapt from one tree to the next, roaring hungrily. The breeze carried the rank smell of burned-out ground and charred forest.

Showers of orange sparks began to streak past them. Lisa cried out as a burning windblown piece of moss hit her shoulder. She batted it out.

The tallest of the trees on the ridgeline became a torch, orange against the smoky-gray sky. Then it swayed, creaked, groaned, and began to tip. Toward them.

"It's coming down!" Wyatt yelled. "Hurry!"

"But it's too far away," Natalia protested. Even if it did fall, wouldn't it just land on the loose rocks covering the hill?

She didn't have it in her to run. She barely had it in her to walk. Still, she managed to pick up her pace to a shuffling jog.

With a sound that eclipsed even the hungry roar of the flames, the burning tree crashed with a bang on the steep scree slope behind them. Even through the soles of her boots, she felt the impact. Behind her, Beatriz swore in Spanish.

Natalia turned to see why. Her stomach bottomed out. *No*, she thought. *No, please, God, I'm not seeing this.*

The tree, still coated in flames, had landed pointing downhill. But instead of coming to a rest, it began to slide with a terrible grinding noise. The two thousand feet of loose rocks, which had been like a no-man's land the fire couldn't cross, now became a liability as, one by one, the burning tree's branches caught and then were torn off.

Each time a branch was ripped away, the tree's trunk moved faster, until finally it was just a giant burning wooden missile.

And it was coming straight toward them.

"Run!" Wyatt shouted, grabbing her hand! "Run!"

## CHAPTER 27

# CRASHING DOWN

7:13 A.M.

**"RUN!" WYATT YELLED AGAIN.**

*Crack! Clack!* On the scree slope above them, the burning log was shoving rocks out of its path with a sound like thunder.

With shouts and screams, everyone scattered. They weren't running to anything, just away from the deadly missile bearing down on them.

Pulling Natalia behind him, Wyatt veered off the trail to the left. On Wyatt's back, Trask was wailing as he jostled up and down.

Natalia ran at a slant, looking back over her shoulder. With horror, she saw the burning log cleave through the underbrush, cutting across the trail they had just been on, leaving fire in its wake. Through the smoke, she saw some of the others trying to scramble out of the way just before the trunk reached them.

AJ was close behind her. A dozen feet farther back, Marco was screaming, "B! B!" as Blue barked frantically.

But Beatriz was nowhere in sight.

Neither were Ryan or Lisa. Or Susan. Or Darryl or Zion.

Far ahead of them came a bang. The burning log had finally run into something big enough to stop it. But it had already done its damage. Only a few hundred feet away, the flames that had sprung up in its wake began to nibble here, take large mouthfuls there.

The forest fire was no longer behind them. It was here.

Hurrying back to Marco, Wyatt grabbed his wrist. "Beatriz must be on the other side of the new fire. We'll catch up with her later. But right now, we all have to get out of here."

Marco gave him a wild-eyed look. But something in Wyatt's words or expression must have gotten through to him, because he turned his back on the flames and started running away.

The fire was already growing. Watching the flickers skitter and flow, swirl and twine, Natalia felt as frozen as she had six years earlier, when she had watched the fire race up the kitchen curtains.

"Natalia! We've got to go! Come on!"

Wyatt's words helped break the spell. She tore her gaze away to turn and follow Wyatt, Marco, and Blue, with AJ at her heels.

Hurtling through the prickly undergrowth with outstretched hands, she tried to protect her face as branches slapped against her palms. Under her feet, small sticks snapped like tiny bones breaking. Her heart was a hammer in her chest and her mouth filled with the flat metallic taste of adrenaline.

Bouncing on Wyatt's back, Trask was kicking and flailing. She reached out to pat him, but he was too wrought up for a random touch to soothe him. A branch whipped her face but she barely felt it.

What had happened to his parents? With their injuries, had Ryan and Lisa been too slow to get out of the way of the log or the fire it had left behind? Was Trask now an orphan? At his age, he would surely grow up with no memory of his parents.

If he grew up at all.

And what about Zion? Had Darryl and Zion moved fast enough?

At the thought of one or both boys dying, it all came crashing down on Natalia. They had come so far and survived so much, and for what? Just to die a few miles short of their destination?

Ahead of her, Wyatt threaded through trees and swerved around clumps of brambles. Now he squeezed between two trees only to be confronted by dense underbrush. He started to back up, then looked over his shoulder, past Natalia, and swore.

Already feeling hollowed out, she turned. The flames were just two hundred yards away. Some were spot fires not much bigger than a human hand waving a frantic warning. Some were jagged lines creeping ever closer, flaring up when they found a new source of fuel. All of them sizzling, snapping, and getting louder by the second. All of them gradually merging into a single conflagration.

With renewed energy, Wyatt turned back and forced his way through the closely packed ground cover. Natalia was following close on his heels when tendrils snagged the laces of her boot. She went sprawling headlong, scratching her face and arms. A big hand appeared in her field of vision. AJ's. Without a word, he pulled Natalia to her feet and they were off again.

Embers trailing thin plumes of smoke began to fall all around them. Some landed on her clothes, peppering them with tiny holes. The roar was rising. Now blizzards of orange sparks flew past them, and then bunches of needles lit up like flares. The air was as hot as a pottery kiln. Natalia's tongue felt fat and swollen against her dry lips, while sweat streamed down her spine. When she wiped her stinging eyes, her palm came away smeared gray with ash.

And then a new smell was layered over the scent of woodsmoke. The sickening stench of burning hair.

A hand slapped her head from behind. Hard. Natalia turned, startled.

"Sorry!" It was Marco. "Your hair was on fire."

"Oh." She hadn't felt a thing. "Thanks."

They raced on, picking their way through a gauntlet of spot fires. The air was starting to tremble. Burning sticks, pine cones, and even branches began raining down all around them. They broke into a thrashing run, stumbling on rocks and brush. Blue galloped alongside, barking as if to encourage them.

Their pace was a compromise between two identical agonies. Too slow and they would burn to death. Too fast and they would trip and fall—and then burn to death.

Natalia imagined what it would be like, their lungs searing, their pack straps melting on their backs as they stumbled their last steps before the fire ate them up.

Finally, they burst through a line of trees. Natalia saw what Wyatt must have been making for. A lake, with a rocky shore.

Ahead of them was a long stretch of water. Behind them a horseshoe of fire.

"Take off your boots, tie them together, and hang them around your neck," Wyatt said between gasps. "We'll need them on the other side of the lake. AJ and Natalia, you're going to have to ditch your packs."

This close to the water, the air had a colder, cleaner sent. Natalia tried to pull it deep into her lungs as she shrugged off her backpack and pulled off her boots. She tied them together and put them around her neck, staring out at the long expanse of smooth water. But every move was just delaying the inevitable.

In his Teva sandals, Marco splashed in. AJ was the first out of his boots and into the lake. Blue launched himself into the water, which was rippling from the wind created by the fire.

"Can you tighten the straps on Trask?" Wyatt asked her. His face was smeared with ash. "I don't need him to go floating off." He said *floating* but she knew he meant *sinking*.

As she tightened the straps she murmured reassurances, her lips close to Trask's ear. He had finally stopped screaming.

"You're okay. It'll be okay." She was saying it as much for herself as she was for him.

But Trask didn't seem to believe her any more than she did. His breathing didn't slow. His chest kept rising and falling in the same too-rapid rhythm. His eyes were swollen, and he seemed too exhausted to cry.

"They're tight." Natalia clapped Wyatt's shoulder.

"Thanks. Now get in the water. Hurry!"

Even though she could feel the hairs on her arms crisping, she wanted nothing more than to collapse. Instead, she shouted the truth.

"I can't swim that far!"

## CHAPTER 28

# EVERYONE ELSE IS DEAD

8:06 A.M.

**WYATT'S EYES WIDENED.** "CAN'T you dog-paddle? That's what I'm going to do, to keep Trask's head out of the water."

Just looking at the wide expanse of water made her feel like the ground was falling away from beneath her feet. "I've never been a good swimmer," she said miserably. "I can't even swim the length of a pool without having to hold on to the side or stand up. And that shore is way farther away than that."

AJ was about twenty feet from shore, moving his legs like egg beaters. Marco was closer in, the water up to his waist. Both of them were looking at her with worried expressions.

More and more embers were falling around them. "We can't stay here, Natalia," Wyatt said. "I know you're scared, but you have to at least get into the water." He held out his hand. "Come on, we'll do it together."

She took his hand and stepped in. The shock of the cold water, such a contrast to the oven-hot air, took her breath away. The rocks under her feet had been worn smooth. Together, they took another step and then a third. Some kind of grasslike plant slid across her calves.

"Everyone else is dead, aren't they?" she said, pitching her voice for Wyatt's ears alone.

"We don't know that." Somehow his voice was still calm. "They ran. We ran. We just picked a different direction, that's all."

"They're probably fine," Marco said in a shaky voice. So much for Natalia thinking the other two hadn't heard.

Another step and another. They were now even with Marco, the water up to their waists. When the water touched his toes, Trask let out a whimper and pulled his knees up higher on Wyatt's back. Smoke was beginning to roll over the lake now, peppered with more flying sparks that hissed when they hit the water. One landed on Marco's bleached hair. He ducked his head and came up coughing.

Behind them, a long limb crashed down, half on the beach and half in the water. Natalia let out a shriek as the very tip of a burning branch traced a path down her upper arm. At first there was just a feeling of surprise. Only when the bright pink line changed to red did she feel the sting of it.

Natalia turned. There were dozens of trees ringing the lake. Maybe hundreds, which meant thousands of tree limbs that could fall. The whole length of the shore was on fire.

She wanted to cry. She couldn't stay here, but there was no way she could make it that long distance.

Above the trees, tongues of burning gases licked fifty feet into the air, topped with coils of black smoke. The flames whipped back and forth as if trying to tear themselves free. Another burning branch fell into the water.

"Natalia!" AJ called. He was still efficiently treading water a dozen yards away. "Take off your pants!"

Had she heard him right? "What?"

"Take off your pants. There's a way to turn them into a life jacket."

Absurdly, Natalia was reminded of high-level math, of how in topology a doughnut was the same as a coffee cup. "I don't understand."

He was swimming back to them, his head out of the water. "It's something they teach in the navy. Hurry!"

The determination in his voice was enough to make her start undoing the button. "You're in the navy?"

"No. But I watch a lot of videos about it. Now stop talking and take off your pants."

AJ believed whatever he was having her do would work. But he had also believed he was having a heart attack, and he'd been wrong about that. Still, what were her choices? Try to swim and drown halfway across? Force the others to leave her and hope to survive long enough for the fire to burn itself out, for the earth to cool down?

Steadying herself on Wyatt's shoulder, Natalia slipped one leg and then the other out of her pants. She was trusting AJ. Trusting him based on a YouTube video.

"Wait, I've heard about this," Marco said. "How you can turn your pants into a flotation device, right? Some German tourist fell off a cruise ship and managed to keep himself alive for three hours in the ocean."

"That's right," AJ said. "Now hand them over."

Natalia did. Even though the guys were probably all past caring, she was glad the water hid her polka-dot underwear and scarred legs.

AJ knotted the ends of the legs twice, then pulled to tighten the knot. Next he buttoned and zipped them. Then he held the waist open between his hands, lifted it over his head, and rapidly brought it down. Like magic, the pants caught air along the way until both legs were swollen with it. Natalia was reminded of the tall windsock cloth tube characters that sometimes danced in front of businesses.

"Yes!" Marco pumped one fist in the air while AJ smiled proudly.

Careful to keep the waistband under the surface of the water so that the air couldn't escape, AJ helped Natalia slip the makeshift life vest over her head. Once the knot was behind her neck, the legs on either side, he passed her the waistband. "Hold this. Then you can float on your back and kick."

Tentatively, Natalia let her head rest on the air trapped inside the pants. When her legs started to float up in front of her, she felt equal parts fear and pride. "Just start kicking," Wyatt said. "I'll tell you if you start moving in the wrong direction." He looked at all of them. "And just to double-check, when I dog-paddle, Trask's head is still out of the water, right?"

He demonstrated for a few strokes, but the toddler's head was well above the waterline. Trask looked too tired to be scared.

"You're good, dude," Marco said. "We'll keep an eye on both of you."

"If something goes wrong, you guys should just think about yourselves," Natalia said. "Not me."

"It's a little late for that," AJ said. "We're a team now."

Tentatively, and then a little harder, she started kicking. What if the air leaked out? What if she accidentally let go? The others, even Blue, kept close to her, although she was sure they could go much faster.

They were facing toward where they were going, but she was looking back to where they had been. The slowly receding shoreline looked more and more like a hellscape. Whole burning trees were toppling into the water where they had been standing not that long ago.

"You're doing great," Wyatt said. "How does Trask look?"

She tore her gaze away from the fire. Trask's head was turned toward her, resting on the back of Wyatt's neck. His eyes were closed. "You won't believe it. I think he's asleep."

Instead of being assured, Wyatt looked worried. "Are you sure he's asleep and not unconscious or something?"

Just then Trask's eyes opened and he looked at Natalia. He still looked relaxed. To him, this must feel like a dream.

"His eyes are open now. I think he's just decided to go with things."

Wyatt looked ahead. "We're about halfway across."

AJ appeared on Natalia's other side, then switched from some much more efficient stroke to a dog paddle. "How are you doing, Natalia?"

"Good if I don't think about how deep it must be."

She tried to give him a smile. "So why do you watch videos about the navy?"

"I've always dreamed of joining up, but it doesn't seem like it's for someone like me. Someone who's out of shape and scared of everything."

"You're a good swimmer."

"I've always liked to swim." His smile was rueful. "And in the water a few extra pounds actually help."

It was easier to feel confident for him than it was for herself. "You can always get in better shape. And I think most people feel scared sometimes. Even petrified. It's like that saying, 'Feel the fear, and do it anyway.'"

"Like you're doing," AJ said.

Before Natalia could answer, Marco started shouting somewhere ahead of them.

"There's people on shore! I see B! She's okay!"

## CHAPTER 29

# SCARS NOW MADE VISIBLE

8:54 A.M.

"YOU CAN STAND UP now, Natalia," Wyatt said. "We've reached the shore."

Still clinging to her makeshift flotation device, she stood up. The water was only waist-deep.

As she turned toward the shore, Ryan and Lisa splashed toward them, calling Trask's name, their arms outstretched.

"We've been so worried." Ryan's voice broke. "I can't believe you swam that whole way! Thank God you're all still alive."

"Let me get Trask out." Lisa's voice broke with urgency. "I just need to hold him, at least for a second." She started fumbling with the straps on Wyatt's back. Trask woke up and reached for her.

Her heart in her throat, Natalia scanned the rocky shore. What about the others? Had they survived?

First she spotted Beatriz. Marco had his arms around her. Her head was tucked underneath his chin. It was another layer of relief to see Beatriz still had Wyatt's backpack, which meant the group still had at least his first aid kit, water bottle, and filter. The two held each other, rocking back and forth, while Blue barked and ran in circles around them. Beatriz's face was smeared with ash, while Marco looked like he had just taken a shower fully clothed.

Behind them were Darryl and Zion. Jumping from foot to foot, Zion was explaining to AJ what had happened.

"The tree just went whoosh past us!" Zion demonstrated by throwing his hands from one side of his body to the other. "Grandpa and I had to run."

Natalia only relaxed when she saw Susan, standing a little apart from the others. The older woman was wringing her hands, looking anxious and confused. But she was alive.

"Come on, Natalia." Wyatt held out his hand from where he stood on the shore. "We need to keep moving."

The whole time she had been counting heads, her fingers had been working at the knots in her pants, now empty of air. "I need to put my pants back on, but I think the knots are too tight."

He splashed back out to her. "Let me try." After tugging and fiddling, Wyatt even tried using his teeth. Finally, he swore. "It's like they're superglued."

"I don't exactly want to hike in my underwear."

He pulled the knife from his pants pocket. "How do you feel about shorts?"

"It beats the alternative."

He had her hold the knot while he grabbed a pant leg and sawed away. Eventually, the lightweight nylon cloth parted with a loud ripping sound. When it reached the seam, Wyatt had to give the blade an extra tug. After they repeated the process with the other leg, she slipped into pants that now ended at her knees.

After she stepped out of the water, she saw Ryan wince at her exposed scars. He looked away when he saw her noticing. Did he recognize them for what they were? For a minute, Natalia allowed herself to think about the future, about how they might be rescued, how Ryan and Darryl and Lisa might be treated by real doctors. About how Ryan might learn firsthand the truths behind her scars, about debriding and grafts and skin so tender that at first even the weight of a cotton sheet was too much to bear.

She was still lost in thought when Beatriz wrapped her in a hug. "I'm so glad you're alive. When that burning log split us up, we all freaked out, wondering what had happened to you guys."

"We were doing the exact same thing." Marco slipped his arm around Beatriz's waist as soon as she released Natalia.

"I thought you guys were gone forever," Zion said. "And Wyatt's the only one who knows where to go."

As if to underscore Zion's words, Wyatt had already pulled the map from his pocket and unfolded it. Instead of being a waterlogged mess with disintegrating paper and smeared ink, it looked untouched.

"That survived the swim?" Natalia asked.

"It's printed on waterproof paper. I wish I could say the same for my phone." He tapped a spot on the map. "So anyway that's Knox Lake we just crossed. Even though the fire may not be able to get across, it's already working its way around the lake. But if we keep ahead of it, we can pick up the Cougar Creek trail."

"Wait a minute," Darryl said. "Haven't we just spent the better part of a day avoiding the Cougar Creek fire?"

Wyatt shrugged. "That was when we were miles farther north, where there's still active fire. But I think we should head to where the fire started a couple of weeks ago. The fire already burned everything there and then moved on. If you can't outrun a forest fire, then the best place to be is in what smoke jumpers call 'the black.' Because things can't burn twice."

"And if we do that, if we take the Cougar Creek trail, how much farther to civilization?" Marco asked.

"Once we meet up with Cougar Creek, it looks like it's only about three miles to a road."

*Road.* It almost sounded like a foreign word to Natalia. The reality of the last twelve hours—of running for her life over and over, of near misses and panic, of one injury or problem after another, of exhaustion sapping the strength from her muscles—seemed like just how things worked now. It was hard to imagine ever breathing clear air again, or licking her lips and not tasting ash, or lying down between crisp white sheets. Hard to imagine finally being safe.

AJ, Wyatt, and Natalia put their wet boots back on. Then Lisa placed Trask back in the carrier Wyatt was still wearing. While people took turns drinking lake water through Wyatt's filter, AJ said, "Here, Susan, let me carry your pack for you a bit."

She took a step back. "You don't need to do that."

"I know I don't need to. I want to. Plus, I don't feel right without something on my back, and I had to leave my pack on the other side of the lake."

Even though her expression betrayed that she wasn't quite following him, she still started to shrug out of the straps. As she did, she looked down at her arms. "What happened to my arms?"

He answered patiently. "You just scratched them up a bit last night. But you're okay." He settled the straps over his own shoulders.

At first the woods ahead of them were untouched, but soon there were scattered burned patches where sparks had fallen but not found enough fuel to stay alive.

They had been hiking for about a half hour when they heard the burble and mutter of water flowing over rocks. Then the woods opened up and they saw the source. A stream. While it was only about fifteen feet wide, the water looked at least thigh-deep.

And it was moving fast.

## CHAPTER 30

# SUCK YOU UNDER

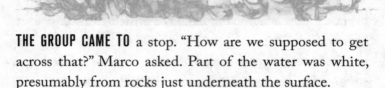

**THE GROUP CAME TO** a stop. "How are we supposed to get across that?" Marco asked. Part of the water was white, presumably from rocks just underneath the surface.

"Isn't there some kind of bridge we could use?" Lisa appealed to Wyatt.

He was checking his map. "We're off-trail now, so there isn't a crossing anywhere nearby. I think we're going to just have to figure out the best place to ford it."

"It doesn't look that deep." Ryan narrowed his eyes. "That lake you guys got across was way deeper."

"Yeah," Wyatt said, "but this is moving water, not still. Which means physics are not in our favor. Water weighs something like sixty pounds per cubic foot. If it's moving, the pressure increases with the square of its velocity."

Darryl tilted his head. "Can you say that in plain English?"

"It means that if the water is moving twice as fast in one section as in another, then it's exerting four times as much force. If it's moving ten times as fast, that's ten times ten, or one hundred times the force. It's tempting to cross where it's narrowest, but then the water will be deeper and faster. And the deeper the water is, the more we'll float, which means it's harder to stay upright. We want to find the shallowest, slowest part."

AJ grimaced. "Even then, for some people it's going to be tough."

Wyatt was looking at each of them in turn, weighing how difficult it would be. "We'll have the strongest people form a human chain, and then we'll have the others go over one at a time in front of the chain. That way if someone loses their footing, the people in the chain will catch them. After they're done, the rest of us will finish going across." He took a deep breath. "But it's worth taking a few minutes to look for the best place. And that includes making sure there's nothing immediately downstream that someone might run into if they get swept away."

"Like a waterfall?" Beatriz asked. "That always happens in movies."

Wyatt nodded. "Exactly. Or something like that that boulder." He gestured at a big gray rock shouldering out of the water. "That could break a bone or knock someone unconscious."

Ryan pointed upstream. "What about where it turns? It looks calmer there."

Wyatt pinched his lips between index finger and thumb as he considered it. "It does, but sometimes that means there are deep pools or undercurrents. It's all a trade-off. A straight stretch might have faster water, but it's also more likely to be a consistent speed and have a flat bottom."

He kept walking downstream while the others followed

in a strung-out, exhausted line. Finally he found a spot he liked. "What about here?" In the middle of the water was a tiny island, about two feet across. A few leggy weeds grew from it. "That could give people a resting spot. And with luck, it could mean the current is cut in two and weaker on both sides. I'll check it out first."

Before going across, Wyatt asked to borrow Lisa's trekking pole. She gave it to him and then lifted Trask out while Wyatt borrowed the other pole from Susan.

"Should you take off your shoes?" Marco asked.

"That made sense when we were swimming and didn't want to get weighted down. But going across the stream barefoot means it is easier to slip and fall—or just hurt your feet."

Wyatt scrambled down the bank until he was standing next to the water. When he stepped in, rather than cutting straight across, he faced upstream and began shuffling sideways at a diagonal. Natalia's breath went shallow as she watched him test each step, first with the pole and then his foot. Carefully, he began to cross, making sure one foot was planted before moving the next one. At the center, it was a little less than three feet deep—but that would be chest-deep for Zion.

Once Wyatt got to the other side, he reversed the process, still moving deliberately and carefully. After he got out of the water, he didn't climb back up the bank. "The current's definitely pushy, but the bottom is rocky and didn't feel too slippery. I say we go for it." While they jumped or gingerly picked their way down the three-foot-high bank to the narrow shore, he looked them over, and one by one they joined him on the shore. "For the chain, let's have me, AJ, Natalia, Beatriz, and end with Marco. Then the rest of you can cross in front."

Darryl puffed out his chest. "I can be part of the chain."

"We need you to go over with Zion. It's going to be the hardest on him."

"What about Trask?" Lisa asked. "Who's going to carry him?"

Natalia realized that none of the choices were good. The people on the chain were the strongest, but also at the most risk. That left Zion, Darryl, Susan, Lisa, and Ryan.

"I'll do it," Ryan said.

"No," Lisa said. "Your shoulder is burned."

Ryan shrugged. "Just on the outside. Not where the straps hit."

"Wait a minute," Wyatt said. "I haven't been thinking straight. If anyone falls into the water, the best way to survive is to shed your pack, get on your back, and point your feet downstream. But you obviously can't do that if you have a baby on your back."

"My sister was big into wearing her kids," Beatriz said, untying her beach towel–turned–cape. "I think it's possible to use this to tie Trask to Ryan's front."

It took a few tries for Beatriz to remember how it was done, but eventually the towel was snugged under Trask's butt and wrapped around Ryan's torso, and the ends of the towel were tied around his unburned shoulder.

After putting back on the empty child carrier, Wyatt had them link arms on the narrow shore. "We'll be moving on my count at an angle so we can help break the current for the person behind us. Don't cross your legs. Just keep shuffling sideways."

Was he afraid? Natalia couldn't tell. Since he was in the lead, he would be bearing the brunt of the current. Feeling each step with the pole, he waded back into the water as he began to call out their steps.

"Left foot. Right foot. Left. Right."

Natalia's arm was threaded through AJ's on one side and Beatriz's on the other. She stepped into the water. It was immediately as high as her calves. She let out an involuntary gasp at how cold it was. Behind her, she felt Beatriz's arm tighten as she slipped a couple of inches before catching herself. But they kept bulling their way forward, until finally the five of them spanned the width of the stream.

"Good job!" Wyatt called. "Careful not to lock your knees." Then he yelled for Susan to come across. She moved a little uncertainly without her pole but still made it across. Darryl and Zion crossed together. Lisa was next, using the pole to steady herself. Ryan went last. Trask kept patting his dad's face and babbling, but Ryan didn't let himself respond until they were safely on the other side.

Once everyone was across, Marco detached himself and made his way carefully across the stream. One by one, the line unpeeled, until finally only Wyatt was left standing in the stream.

"We did it!" Smiles broke through their exhaustion. Natalia felt her spirits lighten.

Wyatt put Trask on his back again and returned the trekking pole to Susan. Their boots sloshing at every step, the group moved forward in scattered clumps. For once, Marco's Tevas served him well. Beatriz's booties were still on her feet, but looking worse for wear. When they came upon an old fallen log, most went around it. AJ elected to go straight over. He grabbed hold of the stub of a branch poking up from the top, then set his right foot on the curve of the trunk. With a grunt, he pulled himself up until he was standing on top, about three feet off the ground. Bending his knees and swinging his arms, he got ready to jump down on the other side.

Suddenly there was a splintering *crunch* as part of the log gave way. He lurched sideways as his left foot disappeared.

An angry hum filled the air.

AJ desperately yanked his foot free. He fell backward off the log, landing on his butt.

From the hole he had punched in the rotten trunk, tiny yellow bodies began to rise up. First dozens, then hundreds, then possibly thousands massed in a dark and angry swarm around the log that had once held their nest.

"Bees!" AJ yelled.

Shrieking, everyone scattered. Everyone but Zion, who had frozen. And when AJ desperately scrambled to his feet, he accidentally knocked Zion off-balance. Face-first into the log.

Right into the bees' nest.

## CHAPTER 31

# STOP HIS HEART

10:10 A.M.

**WITH A BELLOW, DARRYL** sprinted, not away from the bees, but right into the middle of them. Paying no mind to the angry, buzzing swarm, he leaned down into the middle of it and hoisted Zion in his arms. Holding the boy to his chest, he ran back the way he had come. Barking, Blue followed.

"Everyone else—stop!" Wyatt yelled. "Stay as still as you can! Don't run or wave your arms or try to get them off you. It'll just make them madder."

It took all of Natalia's will to stop running, to stand stock-still when her heart was banging in her chest.

She felt a tiny tap on her cheek as a bee bounced off. *Bees won't hurt you if you don't hurt them.* That's what Natalia's mom had always said. But these bees *had* been hurt. And they were mad. She felt a sting just below the curve of her jaw. Another on her left hand. A third on her right calf.

The bees' buzzing reached a crescendo, like a hundred people angrily humming some avant-garde piece of music, or a machine with something stuck in the gears grinding to a halt.

The only other noise was coming from Trask, who was shrieking.

Natalia didn't move anything but her eyes. A few feet from her, AJ stood frozen mid-stride. Lisa had her hands cupped over her face, while Ryan was looking back over his shoulder. They reminded Natalia of a playground game she had loved in second grade. One person would spin in a tight circle, holding another player by the wrist, and then let go. The goal was to stay as still as a statue in whatever awkward position you ended up.

Slowly, the bees tightened in a dark cloud around their broken home. One by one they began to dip back inside the log.

As soon as she no longer saw yellow forms buzzing past her face, Natalia started to slowly turn in the direction Darryl had carried Zion. When that didn't seem to aggravate the bees, she took a careful step and then another, keeping her torso stiff and her arms at her sides. With each step, she increased her speed, already dreading what she would find.

In a small clearing, Zion lay on his back, his eyes darting with panic. Darryl was murmuring assurances in a shaky voice. He was using a credit card to scrape off the remains of stingers from Zion's ashen face. Bees, Natalia remembered, could only sting once, and then they died.

Had the bees just traded their lives for Zion's?

As she dropped to her knees, the others began to gather around them. All of them were dotted with welts. Trask was still screaming and red-faced, inconsolable even after Lisa hastily pulled him from the child carrier.

If Zion had been stung on the extremities, a reaction might have taken hours. But Natalia counted at least a dozen welts on Zion's face and neck, with more on his hands.

He was already wheezing. It was the same ragged sound Marco had made when he had his asthma attack.

"Now I'm the zombie," Zion said to Marco. His voice rasped and shook.

"I'm sorry, buddy." Marco bit his lip, looking like he was trying not to cry.

"Didn't I tell you not to use his EpiPen?" Darryl demanded. "Now what are we going to do?" Natalia could hear tears in his voice, too.

"Wyatt, do you have any Benadryl in your first aid kit?" Natalia asked. Hers was back on the other side of a lake inside her discarded pack.

"I don't." His face was anguished. "I'm sorry."

"Does anyone have any allergy pills on them?" she asked the others. But she was met only by blank, frightened stares. Even though they probably wouldn't have done much, she would have given anything to have the ones in her first aid kit now. Because Darryl was right. They had gambled with Zion's life—and they were losing.

Zion's wheezing was getting even faster.

"Okay, Zion. Breathe with me." Natalia exaggerated the sound of her breathing and slowed it down, the way she had with AJ. But this wasn't a panic attack. And just like with Marco's asthma, calming him down wouldn't stop the reaction, just slow it down a bit.

It had only been a few minutes since Zion had been

stung, but his lips were already swelling, pushing out from his face, like an actress who had resorted to far too much Botox. Natalia had heard the term *bee-stung lips* before. She had thought it meant what would happen if someone was stung on the lips. But now she understood it must refer to anaphylactic shock.

It wasn't only his lips that were swelling. The hollows under Zion's eyes were puffing up like pillows, pushing his eyes closed. Through the rapidly closing slits, his dark eyes darted back and forth, from Darryl's face to Natalia's.

"Maybe if we hurry we could get him to the road and call an ambulance," Beatriz said.

Nobody answered. They didn't have to. It was clearly just a wish. They were hours from a road. And every second Zion's breathing grew more labored.

"You've killed him. You've all killed him." Darryl pointed at AJ. "You knocked him down." Next his finger pointed at Natalia and then Marco. "And *you* made me use Zion's EpiPen on *him*. And now my grandson's going to die."

"Don't talk like that," Lisa said. "It was an accident. And there has to be something we can do."

"I'm so sorry." AJ's voice shook.

"I would never have let them use the EpiPen if I thought Zion would need it." Marco pushed back his hair from his eyes.

"Wait a minute," Wyatt said. "Do you still have them? The EpiPens?"

"I stuck them in your pack so I could throw them away when we got back. But they're both empty."

"Maybe not," Wyatt said. "A hiking buddy told me once there's actually more than one dose per pen. He said in an emergency it's possible to hack one to get more doses out of it."

"So how do you do it?" AJ asked urgently.

"That's the thing," Wyatt admitted with a grimace. "He didn't give me any specifics."

Marco had already pulled one out of its box. "I'm pretty good at reverse engineering things." His fingers scrabbled at the plastic instructions glued around the clear tube, obscuring the contents.

"Give it to me." Beatriz held out her hand. "I've got longer fingernails." With her now-battered purple-painted nails, she managed to scrape up a corner and then handed it back.

Marco carefully unpeeled the rest. Muttering under his breath, he peered into the translucent plastic housing. One finger traced a line in the air as he tried to figure it out.

Zion began to cough. Even the inhalations between coughs were wrong, squeaking and squealing.

"I don't get why there would be extra medicine," Beatriz said. "EpiPens are so expensive. Why would they waste a single drop?"

Wyatt answered like the engineer he planned on becoming. "Maybe there needs to be an extra volume of liquid in order to create enough pressure to push the right amount through. That's just a guess. But it doesn't matter why it's there. Just that it is. *If* it is."

"I think there might be some left, but it's hard to be sure," Marco said. "I'm going to have to take it apart." He pointed at the back of the EpiPen. "Back here, there's a spring. When you push it against the thigh, the spring forces the needle through clothes and skin and into the muscle. But we don't need it. They were just trying to make it as hands-off and unintimidating to a layperson as possible."

"Whatever you're going to do, hurry," Darryl said. Zion's coughs were getting louder and lasting longer. His swollen face looked almost battered.

"Let me have your knife," Marco said to Wyatt. He unfolded it and handed it over. After resting the tube on a flat stone, Marco poked the tip an inch down from the top. He cut it with a rocking motion, turning it, before he broke the top off with a *pop*. A black spring shot out of the back.

Gingerly, Marco slid out the syringe inside. On top was a covered needle. Inside the bottom of the syringe was a round black piece of rubber. And in between, as Wyatt's friend had said, was more clear liquid and a small amount of air.

Marco pulled off the gray sheath covering the needle. "Okay, that black rubber stopper regulates the dose. If I draw the needle back"—he pointed the needle up until it drew air—"until the plunger is near the end of the glass tube, and then turn it all back over"—he pointed the needle down—"and depress the plunger, it will stop again at the stopper. And it will give the same amount it did originally. It looks like it holds four or five doses."

"Are you sure about this?" Ryan said. "Obviously the manufacturer never intended someone to do that to an EpiPen."

"I'm sure it will give him the right dose," Marco said.

"And obviously the manufacturer also never intended for some kid to"—Wyatt lowered his voice—"die because he got stung by a bee."

"Just do it!" AJ cried out. "Listen to how terrible he sounds! It can't make anything worse than it already is."

"Stop!" Darryl shielded Zion with his body. "What about that bubble? You'll inject him with air. That bubble will stop his heart."

"No, it won't," Natalia said. "This is going into the thigh muscle, not a vein." Darryl didn't look convinced, so she grabbed his hand. "I swear to you, even if there is a bubble of air it won't hurt Zion. But not getting his medicine definitely will."

As if to underline what she had said, Zion let out a strangled cough so awful that all the hairs on Natalia's arms rose.

"Do it!" Darryl said.

Marco wrapped his fingers around the tube and jabbed the needle into Zion's leg. And he pushed the plunger.

## CHAPTER 32

# NOT THE MONSTER

10:19 A.M.

"I CAN'T HEAR HIM anymore," Darryl said frantically. About a minute had passed since Marco injected the epinephrine. "I can't hear Zion breathing!"

Beatriz began to sob in Marco's arms. Lisa clutched Ryan's unburned hand. Susan began to shake her head.

"No!" AJ wailed. "No! I'm so sorry!" He covered his face with his hands.

*Oh God, oh God, no.* Natalia leaned over Zion's still, small form, squinting through the gathering smoke. His face was so puffy that it was hard to tell, but it seemed slack. Lifeless. She turned her head so she was looking toward his feet, her ear brushing Zion's swollen lips. Time expanded as she heard nothing, saw nothing.

Was there any point in trying to give him a second dose? Was he dead? If Zion's airway was completely closed, was there even any point in trying CPR? Chest compressions might be able to force the blood to move around in his body, but that blood wouldn't do him much good if it didn't carry fresh oxygen.

Then a puff of air, warm and moist, touched her cheek.

At the same time, she saw Zion's chest almost impercep-
tibly fall.

Natalia blinked. Had she imagined it? But a second
later his ribs rose a half inch as his lungs expanded.

She realized that just because those horrible harsh
moaning breaths had stopped it didn't mean Zion was
dead. It meant the hacked EpiPen was reversing the anaphylactic shock.

"Zion *is* breathing!" Natalia cried to the ring of worried faces. "The medicine is starting to work." She sat back
on her heels and took her own deep breath. "That's why
we aren't hearing him. Because he's getting better."

Zion's eyes were still swollen into slits, but now he
opened them a fraction.

"Hey, guys." His voice was faint.

Darryl struggled to say something, but was so over-
whelmed with emotion that all he could do was shake his
head. Tears ran down from behind his sunglasses.

"Listen." Zion made an exaggerated breath in and
out, but it was barely audible. "I'm not the monster
anymore."

"No, son." Darryl's voice was rough. "You're not."
Squeezing Zion's hand, he looked from Wyatt to Natalia
to Marco. "Thank you for saving him."

"I'm afraid none of us are quite saved yet." Wyatt said
with a grimace. "We've still got to get into the burned-out
area. The fire's moving pretty fast."

Natalia turned. Wyatt was right. The fire was close
enough she could see it flickering among the trees, hear

it grumbling as it ate its way through brush and berries, ferns and fronds.

When she turned back to Zion, it was also clear the swelling in his face was rapidly subsiding.

Wyatt got to his feet. "Do you think you can walk, buddy?"

After taking another nearly soundless breath, he nodded. "I think so."

"Good!" Wyatt offered his hand and helped him to his feet. As he did, he added, "I don't know about you, Zion, but I really want to go home."

*Home.* The word was almost painful. Something so familiar, so longed for, but also so impossibly far away.

Zion straightened his shoulders. "Let's go." Even if his face still hadn't been swollen, he was hardly recognizable as the nervous little boy who had begun this hike never letting go of his grandpa's hand.

People got to their feet and gathered their things. Marco shouted for Blue, and after a moment, he appeared. Trask's parents buckled him back into the child carrier. AJ put on Susan's pack. Beatriz grabbed the shoulder straps of Wyatt's.

Natalia touched Beatriz's shoulder. "Let me take it for a while."

"It's okay." Beatriz's words were undercut by the groan she made when she lifted it.

"I know you can do it, but I also know I probably weigh thirty pounds more than you."

"Let her do it, B," Marco said. "That pack weighs

nearly as much as you." This time Beatriz didn't resist when Natalia reached for it.

"Okay!" Wyatt finished checking his map and compass. "That way." He pointed.

Giving the log with the bees' nest a wide berth, they went deeper into the black. At first there were only a few scorched patches, but the farther they went, the blacker it got, until finally they were walking over coal-black earth topped with crumbling ash. The lush green forest had been replaced by dozens of blackened spires, like the masts of wrecked ships.

Every step kicked soot into the air, releasing the reek of burned-out ground and charred wood. Soon they looked like coal miners with black-smudged faces, the whites of their eyes startling amid the grime. Blue occasionally yipped in pain as he found a hot spot.

"Watch out for those." Wyatt pointed at a place where wisps of smoke rose from the forest floor. "Sometimes a root can smolder underground for weeks. If you stepped on one, you could melt your shoes."

"Still beats trying to outrun the fire," Ryan said. His bandages were as filthy as his skin. The one on his shoulder looked wet, like the burn was weeping. While there were a few more bandages in Wyatt's first aid kit, Natalia decided it was better to leave things alone.

They went up a small rise. At the top, they saw four things.

One was a clear line where the burn ended, black on one side and green on the other.

The second was the reason for the demarcation. The

line was actually a narrow slot canyon with a river at the bottom.

The third was Jason.

He was standing in front of the fourth thing. A thirty-foot-long footbridge spanning the canyon.

What was left of the bridge, anyway. Because it had been burned.

## CHAPTER 33

# JUST SCARED

10:34 A.M.

**WHEN HE CAUGHT SIGHT** of the group, Jason started backing away. He was moving awkwardly, his right hand cupping his left elbow. Dangling from his right index finger was the canister of bear spray.

"Don't get any closer!"

They were about thirty feet away. Jason's voice sounded hoarse, which made sense given the smoke and his probable lack of water. But was it also edged with tears?

Ryan snorted. "Trust me, Jason—if that's even your name—we don't want to get close to you at all."

"What happened to your arm?" Zion asked. He was the only one who didn't look some version of angry.

"I tripped. I tripped on a stupid rock, and I fell. Pretty sure my collarbone is broken." The corners of Jason's mouth pulled down. "I can hear it clicking when I try to move it. Like, inside the bone."

His self-diagnosis sounded right to Natalia. It was a common result of what doctors called a FOOSH—*Falling On Outstretched Hand*, the most frequent mechanism of injury.

"What did you think was going to happen when you ran off in the dark?" Sarcasm colored AJ's voice.

"No wonder you took off." Darryl's hands curled into fists. "We figured out you're the one who started the fire."

Jason shook his head vehemently. "Not on purpose."

"Right," Beatriz sneered. "That's why you were carrying around the cap to a road flare."

"And after you realized I'd seen it," Natalia said, "you tried to push me off the bridge."

Jason's mouth twisted. "I was just scared, okay? And I didn't really know you then. I was afraid you were going to tell everyone and they'd figure out the fire was my fault. And then at Sky Bridge you were right in front of me and I just had this sudden, stupid impulse." He sucked in a breath. "But I'm also the one who pulled you back."

Wyatt made a scoffing noise. "You know those two don't cancel each other out, right?"

"And where does that pin covered with diamonds and rubies come in?" Marco asked.

"It was supposed to be the easiest job ever." Jason made a face. "There's this museum out in the middle of nowhere, right? It actually used to be some rich guy's house. A rich guy who had rich friends, including the queen of freaking Romania. And my friend Brian knows a guard there. He said if we came at closing time we could tie him up to make it look good, smash the case, take the jewels, and then later break them apart and sell them. Split everything three ways."

"You said jewels," Ryan said. "So where are the rest?"

"In Brian's pockets." Jason pressed his lips together. "Afterward, I was supposed to set the car on fire so that there wouldn't be any prints or DNA or anything. But something inside exploded. And suddenly everything was on fire, and I had to run." He sounded exhausted. "And now I'm sure Brian's on the plane to Thailand. I doubt he waited for me. We were going to be rich, kicking back on a beach. Instead, I'm stuck in the wilderness. And what good is a seventeenth-century diamond-and-ruby brooch out here?"

Lisa swore. "My husband's got second-degree burns because of you. He should be in a hospital right now. Just like I need a doctor for my knee. Except, we're all trapped in the woods trying to outrun a forest fire. We could all die. Even my baby!" She took one stiff-legged step toward him.

Releasing his elbow, Jason raised the bear spray. "Back off!"

Marco moved to stand beside her. "You do realize there's way more of us than of you, right?"

Ryan stepped up on the other side of his wife.

With a defiant shout, Jason pressed the nozzle, emitting an angled spray of red droplets. Even though everyone started to back up, it didn't matter. The spray went less than fifteen feet.

Meanwhile, Wyatt had started sprinting in a wide circle around the spray, with Trask bouncing and wailing on his back. Wyatt cocked his fist, but rather than punch Jason in the face, he punched him in the upper arm. On the side of the broken collarbone.

With a scream, Jason toppled over, landing on his

back. Wyatt kicked the bear spray away as Marco, Beatriz, and Darryl pinned his legs. While Jason whimpered, Wyatt used the parachute cord to tie his ankles together.

After Wyatt finished, it was like the last bit of fight had gone out of Jason. He lay on his back, cradling his arm and moaning. His eyes were closed, but moisture shone around them. Natalia took a quick look at his collarbone, just long enough to ascertain that it was broken and it wasn't going to kill him.

"Now what?" Marco asked as she did.

"Now we've got two problems," Wyatt said. "How to get across the canyon and what to do about Jason. Since he's not going anywhere, let's figure out the canyon first."

Lisa and Ryan tried to calm Trask while the others ignored the trussed-up Jason, walking past him to stare down at the canyon and what was left of the bridge once spanning it.

All that remained was the metal skeleton. On the other side of the chasm, tantalizingly close, was the trail, a clear path through untouched trees. But in between was a sixty-foot drop. At the bottom was a narrow river, the water churning and white. The walls of the slot canyon both contained the river and increased its power by concentrating it.

"It's like Sky Bridge without the gate," Natalia said.

Lisa shook her head. "It's like Sky Bridge without the bridge."

"So near and yet so far," Beatriz said. The gap was only about thirty feet wide. But it might as well have been thirty miles.

"What are we going to do now?" Darryl sounded exhausted. "We can't get over that."

AJ looked back at the fire. "Well, we can't go back."

"Could we just wait here to be rescued?" Beatriz asked. "They have to be looking for us."

"For all the authorities know, we got burned up last night," Wyatt said. "It's going to take a long time for them to figure out where everyone is. Besides, I don't think we can really afford to wait."

Natalia snuck a glance at Zion. While his face was much less swollen, it was still puffy. If he started to get worse—which she knew was a possibility—they could try giving him one more dose from the EpiPen. But that was it. An overdose of epinephrine could kill him just as easily as could anaphylactic shock.

"Has anyone tried their phones recently?" Lisa said hopefully. But when they checked, nearly all of them were completely dead: battery drained or killed by the swim across the lake. Only Ryan's and Darryl's phones still powered on. And both of them showed "No Service."

"It's not that far to the trail, really," Wyatt said slowly. "All we need to do is get on the other side."

"What do you mean, 'all we need to do'?" Ryan echoed. "Unless we suddenly sprout wings, it's impossible."

Wyatt's eyes traced the lines of the bridge. "It's not like it's totally gone." It was true the metal framework was still there. But the wooden floorboards and sides had burned up, leaving just a series of open metal squares, each about six feet on a side. Each square was braced diagonally by another piece of steel. Taken together, the diagonal braces made a zigzag pattern the length of the bridge.

"Yeah, but the important parts are gone." Darryl's laugh was like a bark. "The parts that you *walk* on."

"But the framework's steel, and it survived," Wyatt said. "It's still got the handrails and the bottom chords of the truss—the pieces that run parallel to the handrails. It's still got the diagonals and the cross struts that were the floor beams." Each of the pieces he named was about six inches wide.

Marco shook his head. "Who cares if it has the floor beams? It doesn't have the actual floor!"

As if he hadn't heard, Wyatt said, "If we held on to the top chord—the handrail—and shuffled along the bottom chord, then we could step around the posts and the braces and get to the other side."

"That's a pretty big if." AJ looked pale. "Look at how far down it is. One missed step and you'd die."

"Let me think this through." Wyatt unbuckled the strap of the child carrier and set it down between Lisa and Ryan. "Maybe we could do it like this." Setting his right foot on the bottom chord, toes facing away from the bridge, he grabbed on to the handrail. He stepped up with the other foot.

Even though at that point the drop beneath his feet was less than a yard, it felt like someone had just put a hand around Natalia's heart and squeezed. He leaned forward over the hip-high handrail, bent at about a forty-five-degree angle, and rested his hands lightly on either side.

Wyatt took a sideways step and then moved his trailing foot to meet the first. Two more shuffling steps brought him to the point where the first post, diagonal, and cross strut met at the bottom chord. He lifted his right foot and carefully placed it on the other side of the post, leaving room for his left to join it.

Her hand across her mouth, Natalia barely breathed as he inched farther and farther away. Moving carefully but quickly, Wyatt made it all the way to the far side of the bridge in less than two minutes. Jumping off, he raised his fists in triumph. His *whoop* carried clearly to them. Instead of answering with their own cheer, the people on the near side of the bridge just tossed anxious glances back and forth. Then Wyatt stepped back up on the bridge, reversed direction, and sidestepped over to them.

"Guys! We can definitely do it!"

Natalia was already shaking her head. "No. I don't think I can do that." She took a step back. "Everyone will just have to go on without me."

## CHAPTER 34

# VIGILANTES

10:46 A.M.

"**I'M WITH NATALIA.**" **AJ** looked pale. "It's too dangerous. One wrong step and that would be all she wrote."

"I swear it's not that hard. The handrail's really solid, and you can lean your hips into it."

When she looked at the skeleton of the bridge, Natalia didn't see the sturdy bones Wyatt had felt comfortable scampering across. She saw the open spaces in between.

Darryl snorted. "Not that hard for *you*. You're an eighteen-year-old Eagle Scout in great shape." He waved his hand to indicate the rest of them. "But we've got old people, kids, folks who are injured . . . even a dog."

After a moment's silence, Wyatt held out his hand. "Marco, can I see the leash?"

Marco unslung it from around his neck and handed it to him. Blue trotted over as if expecting Wyatt to clip it to his collar. He sat down, raised his head, and waited expectantly.

Wyatt grabbed the leash in his fists and pulled hard. It was round, about three-quarters of an inch thick, black with a white reflective thread spiraling around it. One end had a padded handle, and the other was finished with a silver clip.

"This feels a lot like a climbing rope." After feeding the clip end through the handle to make a circle, he hooked it to his belt loop. He gave an experimental tug, then pulled hard enough the muscles in his arm stood out. "Maybe we could use this to clip ourselves to the bridge?"

"But not everyone's got belt loops," Beatriz said, examining the smooth waistband of her shorts.

Wyatt found the flaw in his own idea. "Even if they did, it would mean undoing and redoing it every time you reached a post." He counted. "Six times."

"That's five times too many," Darryl shook his head. "It would be too easy for someone to lose their balance any time they unclipped themselves. And I'm not having my grandson out there by himself, fumbling with the only thing that's keeping him from falling off those pieces of metal that used to be a bridge."

Wyatt looked down at the loop he had made with the leash. "How about this? What if I put the leash around each person's waist, clipped them to me, and then escorted them over? And if for some reason they slipped, they'd still be clipped to me and I could help them regain their balance."

"So it'd be like belaying someone on a rock wall," Ryan said.

"Exactly." Wyatt nodded.

Ryan grunted. "Except the belayer always has his feet on the ground. He's not climbing the wall right next to you. What's to stop both of you from falling off?"

"I'll be holding on to the handrail the whole time."

Wyatt sounded confident. "And so will the other person. The leash is just a precaution."

"That means you'd be going back and forth a dozen times." Beatriz pointed out. "Are you sure you're up for that?"

Wyatt shrugged. "Heights don't really bother me."

AJ ran his hand down his face, still dotted with bee stings, and then sighed. "I think it's the best plan we're going to come up with. And even though I don't like the idea at all, I trust Wyatt. He's gotten us this far."

Most of the others nodded or were at least silent as they weighed their bad choices.

"What about Trask?" Lisa demanded. "I will not have you putting his life at risk a dozen times!"

"No worries," Wyatt said. "I'll take him over just by himself once there are people on the other side to watch him."

Marco pointed at Jason with his chin. He was now sitting up, cradling his arm, head down and eyes closed. "We also need to figure out what to do about him."

Darryl straightened his shoulders. "I say we leave him here." His mouth was a grim line. "Leave him here to deal with whatever nature decides to do to him."

Jason lifted his head and opened his eyes as Zion's jaw dropped. He tugged on Darryl's pants. "Grandpa, no!"

Beatriz raised her voice. "We can't do that."

"It would be poetic justice," Lisa said.

"I don't know," Ryan said.

"He's the reason we're all here," AJ said. "But even so . . ." His voice trailed off.

Only Susan was quiet, her eyes going from speaker to speaker. But her expression was quizzical, like they were all speaking a foreign language.

"Look." Wyatt raised his hands. "When we get to safety, we'll let law enforcement figure out what should happen to Jason. We're not a bunch of vigilantes."

"Wyatt's right," Marco said.

Jason spoke up, startling all of them. "No, Darryl's right. Just leave me here. I'm not worth it." His voice cracked. "Plus I can't use my arm."

Natalia corrected him. "A broken collarbone hurts, that's for sure. But if he doesn't have to put his full weight on it or raise it overhead, I think he could get over."

"And Blue?" Marco asked.

They all stared at the dog. He looked from face to face, as if figuring out which person was going to play with him. Then Susan patted her knee and he trotted over. He butted her gently with his head, tilting his head to encourage her to scratch behind his ears.

Wyatt blew air through pursed lips. "I can think of two possibilities. One is we put him in Trask's carrier after Trask is on the other side. The other is I empty a pack and put his rear legs inside."

"Will he sit still for any of that?" Lisa looked skeptical.

Beatriz spoke up. "My sister's kids are always doing weird things to him, like putting him in hats or riding on his back. He just sits there and lets them. So he might sit still for this."

"Whatever we do," Marco said, "I should be the one to

carry him. He's a pretty chill dog, but this is going to be a challenge even for him."

"Then you start figuring out how to carry him and I'll start taking people over." Wyatt turned to Natalia. "Since you don't like heights, I think I should take you first."

"First?" Natalia laughed disbelievingly. "Why?"

"Because the longer you wait, the more scared you'll be." He leaned closer and whispered for her ears alone. "And I need you to show the others it'll work."

## CHAPTER 35

# THE BITTERNESS OF FEAR

10:56 A.M.

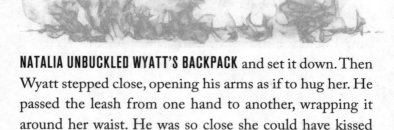

**NATALIA UNBUCKLED WYATT'S BACKPACK** and set it down. Then Wyatt stepped close, opening his arms as if to hug her. He passed the leash from one hand to another, wrapping it around her waist. He was so close she could have kissed him, but only a small part of her mind registered that. The rest was too numbed by fear to think.

By threading the clip through the handle, he again made a lasso, which he pulled snug around her waist. Then Wyatt fastened the leash to his belt loop and stepped back. There was about eighteen inches of leash between them.

"See if that holds."

She tried to step farther back, but the leash wouldn't let her. Next she dropped to her knees. The leash stretched tight, holding her suspended just above the ground.

Taking her hand, Wyatt pulled her back to a standing position. "Let's go."

And before Natalia could argue she wasn't ready or someone else should be first, Wyatt was walking to the bridge and she was following.

He stepped out on the bottom chord, leaving just

enough room for her. As she joined him, a jolt of fear ran up her spine.

Mirroring Wyatt, she rested her forearms on the handrail, cupping her hands around the edge, hinging at the waist so her hip bones pressed into the warm metal edge. It didn't feel as precarious as it had looked when she was watching Wyatt. But of course, it was easy to think that when she could simply reverse course and jump back down on the ground.

"Okay, here we go." He took a sideways step.

Tugged along by the leash, Natalia followed. She was sweating so much that her shirt clung to her back like plastic wrap.

Another step. "You're doing great!" Wyatt said.

His words were more like distant sounds. Natalia's focus had narrowed to the two strips of sun-heated metal—one underneath her feet and one under her hands—that were the only things between her and death.

After two more sets of sideways steps, Wyatt said, "Okay, here's the first post. I'm going to step around and then I'll help you over." When he did, the leash went tight, cutting into her waist. "Now put your hand here." Gently grasping her wrist, he guided her right hand to the correct spot. "That's good. It's just on the other side of the post. Great. Now move your right foot."

A whimper escaped her clenched teeth as she carefully transferred herself to the far side of the post. Her boots felt so stiff and unwieldy. Stiffness had been good for walking over rocks and roots, but now when she needed to maintain contact with the bottom chord it was a drawback.

"You're doing great, Natalia. You really are."

Wyatt kept shuffling sideways and she kept following, even though each step was taking her farther away from safety. Her palms were so wet they slipped along the handrail. What if she completely lost purchase? What if just thinking about slipping off was making it more likely she *would* slip?

Wyatt's voice was as calm as a hypnotist's. "Try focusing your gaze on your hands or maybe your feet."

But it was all too easy to look past her hands or feet. To look past them to white waters where she would die. His words reminded her of Dr. Paris. "Five things you can see," she muttered to herself.

"What'd you say?" Wyatt asked. They were already at the next post. She resisted the crazy urge to turn to look at the empty space behind them. It felt like a vacuum sucking at her. Like an open airlock on a space ship.

"I'm trying to do that thing my therapist taught me, where you find five things you can see, four you can touch, three you can hear, two you can smell, and one you can taste." Gradually, they were falling into a rhythm, like a sideways sack race. His right foot, his left together with her right, then her left.

"Okay, then tell me five things you can see."

"The handrail, the post we just passed, your hand"— she was already running out of things it was a good idea to look at closely—"the ashes smeared on your skin, and um, the bee sting on your wrist."

"We're more than halfway there," he said as they

stepped around another post. "So four things you can touch?"

She forced herself to think. "Your hand. The leash. The post. And I can feel how heavy my boots are."

For a second, he squeezed her hand, and then moved it past another post. "Three things you can hear?"

"My breathing. Your breathing." Hers was too fast, his slow and steady. "Um, and far away, I can hear the fire. And I don't know if this counts, but I can even hear my own heart beating in my ears."

"We've only got one more post. And I didn't even get a chance to ask you about smell and taste."

"I think right now neither one of us should focus on smells." She could smell them both, her body odor a sour note to Wyatt's sharp and spicy scent.

"Fair point."

And her tongue was still coated with the bitterness of fear, even though they had reached the end of the bridge.

"Okay. We made it! Good job! Want to jump off together?"

Natalia was not capable of jumping. She set one foot on solid ground, then the other. Her knees went weak and she felt herself began to sag. Suddenly Wyatt's arms were wrapped around her for real, holding her up. Holding her close.

"You did it," he whispered. "I'm so proud of you. You—"

And then he couldn't talk anymore because Natalia was kissing him. His mouth was soft and hard at the same time. She felt herself catch fire. His teeth bumped hers. She put her hands on either side of his face.

From the other side of the bridge came the sounds of clapping and cheering, even a whistle. They barely registered.

Finally the two of them broke for air, both of them breathing heavily. Natalia wondered if her eyes looked as glazed as Wyatt's did.

After a long moment, he undid the leash from his belt, then slipped it off her.

In a halfway decent Terminator impression, Wyatt growled, "I'll be back."

## CHAPTER 36

# INTO THE EMPTY AIR

### 11:03 A.M.

**AFTER WYATT RETURNED TO** the bridge, a wave of dizziness crested over Natalia. She braced her hands on her knees to keep from tipping over. Her breathing was too fast. But she couldn't tease out how much was from crossing the bridge—and how much from Wyatt's kiss.

By the time she finally gathered herself enough to straighten up, Wyatt was already halfway back with AJ. Even though crossing the bridge had felt endless, she realized it couldn't have taken more than a minute or two. Once AJ was on the other side, he gave her a sweaty hug that lifted her off her feet.

After AJ, Wyatt brought over Zion and then Darryl. Each was greeted with more hugs. Next was Trask. Because he was in the child carrier, it took even less time.

As he undid the carrier's waist strap, Wyatt came over to Natalia.

"Can you watch him while I take back the carrier to see if Blue will fit in it? Beatriz and Marco won't let me bring them over until they're sure Blue can go, too." He made a face. "And I'm going to bring Jason last. I don't want him scampering off without us again."

Natalia helped Wyatt set the carrier down and then undid the chest strap. As she did, Trask startled awake. He began to fuss, rubbing his screwed-up eyes with his fists. She pulled him free. The bottom of his overalls bulged alarmingly, and he smelled strongly of pee. When they made it back to civilization, he would probably have one hell of a diaper rash.

"It's okay, Trask." Setting him on her hip, she began lightly bouncing him up and down, ignoring the squishy sounds it created. Through some alchemy it was no longer painful to look at him. To hold him. He still reminded her of Conner, but the pain had been leached away.

Twisting up his face, Trask stiff-armed her. Pretty much everything was wrong in his universe. No food, bee stings, little sleep, a wet diaper, being carted around by strangers. He had been remarkably resilient, but everyone reached a breaking point.

On the other side of the bridge, Beatriz and Marco, with some assistance from Lisa, were already stuffing Blue into Trask's child carrier. They managed to get him more or less into it, but as soon as they attempted to hoist him onto Marco's back, his rear legs started to scrabble. They pulled him free.

Meanwhile, Wyatt was guiding Susan across. Her eyes were darting around, her lips moving, but Natalia couldn't hear what she was saying. Wyatt kept up a quiet string of assurances.

They were two-thirds of the way across when Susan abruptly stopped. Instead of sliding along, her right foot stepped back from the bottom chord and found only air. She started to tip sideways. The leash pulled taut.

With a shout that echoed back from the steep sides of the canyon, Wyatt grabbed Susan's upper arm with his left hand while his right arm hooked over the handrail.

Natalia watched, frozen. She wasn't breathing. It felt like even her heart stopped beating.

But somehow Wyatt got Susan to shift her body until both her feet were on the bottom chord. At his urging, they began moving again. Still, Natalia didn't take a full breath until the two of them were safe on her side.

Wyatt began to unwind the dog leash from Susan's waist. Susan made no effort to help him, her hands dangling at her sides. She seemed lost. Not in her own thoughts, but lost even to herself. Afterward, she let the others hug her, but it was clear by her expression she didn't understand why, or even who they were.

Before Wyatt went back, his eyes briefly met Natalia's. The look they exchanged said more than words could have. Her look said she was afraid, and his reassured her, and both of them acknowledged they couldn't stand to lose the other.

And then Wyatt stepped back up. On the other side, Marco and Beatriz were emptying out Susan's pack.

Natalia was the last to hug Susan, an awkward sideways hug because she was holding Trask. Releasing the older woman, she said, "Are you okay, Susan?"

"I guess so." Her brow creasing, Susan looked down at

her forearms, dotted with scabs. "What happened to my arms?"

As Natalia explained for the dozenth time, Marco and Beatriz managed to fit the bottom half of Blue inside Susan's pack. He seemed calmer now that his feet had purchase. Beatriz and Lisa helped Marco lift the pack onto his back. Half curled up, Blue faced forward, both front feet resting on Marco's right shoulder.

By then, Wyatt was waiting for Beatriz. After hugging Marco, she let Wyatt wrap the leash around her waist. In ninety seconds, she was on the other side greeting the ones who had crossed before her.

Back with Marco, Wyatt threaded the leash under the backpack and around Marco's waist as everyone fell silent. What if Blue freaked out mid-span? Wyatt had been strong enough to pull Susan back up, but could he pull the weight of a man and a dog? Or what if Blue decided he needed to be free of the pack and leapt?

As they started across, Beatriz pressed her fist against her mouth, biting the side of her index finger. But Blue never shifted on Marco's back. He didn't look anxious, just resigned. Even once Marco was on the other side of the bridge, Blue waited patiently to be freed from the backpack.

Carrying Susan's empty pack, Wyatt made his way back once more. Only Lisa, Ryan, and Jason were left. Ryan and Lisa were pointing at each other. It was clear Ryan wanted his wife to go first, while she was arguing the opposite. Natalia's stomach growled. She let herself think ahead. In two hours, they could be back in civilization. In two hours, they could be eating. Even the thought of stale hospital saltines filled her mouth with water.

Ryan won the argument. While Jason started refilling Susan's pack after Wyatt pointed at it, Wyatt put on the empty child carrier with the trekking pole dangling from it, and then began to shepherd Lisa over, more slowly than he had any of the others. She grimaced each time she had to put full weight on her right knee.

Trask had been sunk is his own miserable torpor, but suddenly he stiffened in Natalia's arms.

"Mama! Mama!" Screaming, he started to thrash. "Mama!"

It was like trying to hold a live eel. He began to slide from Natalia's grasp and down her leg. She tried to shift her grip, but he just slipped free, landing on his butt with a wet plop. He turned over, pushed himself to his feet, and began to run toward the bridge as fast as his short legs allowed . . .

Already off-balance, Natalia desperately lunged for him. But Trask was a moving target and she fell short. The tips of her fingers only brushed him before she hit the ground hard.

Trask kept running straight toward his mother, arms outstretched. Lisa was just behind Wyatt, about ten feet from the end of the bridge.

"Mama!" he wailed. "Mama!"

"No, Trask!" Lisa shouted. "No!"

Everyone was now screaming at him to stop, but Trask's only goal was to reach his mother. Arms reaching for her, he ran the length of the first diagonal, which was about six inches wide. He took two steps on the second before he realized where he was. He looked down. And froze.

He stood teetering. Everyone else had also gone silent and rigid. They only had eyes for the toddler, and the deadly drop below his feet.

Natalia screamed, but only inside her head. In reality, she didn't make a sound. If she startled Trask and he turned, he would surely slip and fall to his death.

Which he was going to do anyway. It was just a matter of time.

Without making a decision, Natalia jumped to her feet. She started to sprint.

Trask took a step back, away from the drop he could see in front of him. A step back into the empty air.

Natalia's feet danced over the first diagonal.

Just as Trask began to drop like a stone from the second.

For an odd, warped moment time stretched out. Then it began to tear.

And in that moment, Natalia launched herself into a dive.

## CHAPTER 37

# HER FATE

11:24 A.M.

**HER HANDS OUTSTRETCHED, NATALIA** dove through the air. A scream trailed behind her like a spent comet.

Time slowed to a crawl. Her senses picked out every detail of what was happening. The colors were impossibly bright, sounds a smear.

*Tick.* Trask began to drop into the triangle formed by the crossbeam, the diagonal, and the bottom chord.

*Tick.* In slow motion, his small hands started to rise above his head. Pudgy fingers spread wide.

*Tick. Now,* Natalia told herself. *Now.* She shaped her hands like *C*s.

*Tick.* The webs between her fingers and thumb made contract with Trask's sweaty wrists.

*Tick.* Her fists clamped closed.

*Tick.* She landed hard on her belly across a metal beam.

*Tick.* Deep inside her chest something snapped.

Suddenly, time resumed its normal pace. Natalia lay facedown, folded in half across a crossbeam, holding a dangling Trask above a sixty-foot drop to churning white water.

And Trask's weight was slowly pulling her down.

"No!" Lisa screamed. "Not my baby!"

Natalia's heart had been replaced by a cold fist of horror. She already knew how this would end.

On either side of the bridge, people were screaming and shouting, punctuated by Blue's barking. But it was Wyatt's voice, just above her, she paid attention to.

"Natalia, listen to me. There's a diagonal beam right behind you. You should be able to hook your legs under it."

Straightening her legs, she slowly let them rise. As she did, her balance began to shift incrementally toward Trask.

What if Wyatt was wrong? What if she missed the beam? The toddler's weight would make her somersault forward, pulling her off the bridge entirely.

Then first her left thigh and then her right calf made contact with the steel of the diagonal beam. Ignoring the grating in her ribs, she arched her back to press her legs even tighter against the diagonal. The move compressed her diaphragm against the crossbeam, forcing her to breathe shallowly. Pressure was building up in her face. Even in her teeth. Her head felt like a balloon about to pop.

But Natalia's thoughts were only on the child she had to save.

"Trask." Lisa's voice was hoarse with panic. "Don't move, baby. Be still."

But asking him to be still was like asking a horse to walk upright on its hind legs. He started to fuss and kick at the empty air, making his wrists shift in Natalia's fists.

It was all so familiar. Suddenly, she was back in the past. Back in her old house, the one that had burned down six years ago. A child's life in her hands and all her choices bad. Back in the place that haunted her nightmares.

She struggled to draw a breath. There was no fire now, she reminded herself. They had already successfully escaped from it. But the slot canyon she was dangling Trask over was far more dangerous than a fall from a second-story window. If a fifteen-foot drop had killed her brother, what would a sixty-foot fall do to Trask?

"Lisa," Wyatt was saying. "Hold tight. I'm going to unclip myself, put the leash over the rail, and then clip it to you."

A beat later, out of the corner of her eye, Natalia saw Wyatt begin to lower himself onto the second diagonal beam. He moved as carefully as a tightrope walker.

On both sides of the bridge, the others were frantically debating how to save them. But Natalia felt strangely removed from the discussion. They didn't understand this was her fate, the one she had wrongly escaped six years ago. It was all going to happen the same way it had before. The boy would fall from her grasp, and then she would follow him down. Only this time when she let herself fall, she really would die.

*No!* Natalia caught herself. No one was going to die today, not if she could help it. She was no longer a scared eleven-year-old. History was not going to repeat itself in an even more terrible iteration. She couldn't let it. She wouldn't. She couldn't leave Lisa and Ryan childless. She had seen how much her brother's death had damaged her parents. And if she died today, their wounds would burst open again. Would never heal.

Not to mention that she had so much to live for. Including the guy who was now straddling the second diagonal. In one hand he held Lisa's trekking pole.

Her biceps were starting to tremble. "Whatever you're thinking of doing," she said, "hurry."

"I think I can catch the back of his overalls with this." Stretching out on his belly, he wrapped his legs around the beam. "Okay, Trask, try to stay still. We're going to help you, buddy."

He began to slide the trekking pole underneath one overall strap. But three inches from the tip of the pole was a small black circle, a rubber skirt meant to keep it from sinking too deep into the earth. Now as Wyatt tried to slide the pole farther in, the rubber circle got caught on the fabric of the overalls.

Wyatt adjusted the angle and tried to wiggle the pole deeper under the strap. As he did, Trask made a wordless sound of protest. Natalia guessed the tip must be digging into his shoulder.

"Stay still, Trask!" she begged as he twisted in her hands. Lisa's and Ryan's cries echoed hers.

But Trask was too little to think ahead, to know what would happen once he succeeded in getting away from Wyatt's poking pole and Natalia's clinging hands. All he knew was he wanted out.

He kicked harder, setting himself swinging back and forth. Millimeter by millimeter, he was sliding from Natalia's grasp. Her arms felt as weak as spaghetti. Her vision began to spin like water swirling down a drain. She had nothing left. Nothing emotionally. Nothing mentally. Nothing physically.

This was it, then. This was the end.

But it wasn't just Natalia's grasp on Trask's wrists that was shifting each time he kicked. His movements also opened up a gap between his back and his overalls. Suddenly, the trekking pole slid to the far side.

With a roar of effort, Wyatt threw himself forward. And just as Trask slid from Natalia's wrists, he grabbed the far end of the pole.

# CHAPTER 38

# STARTING OVER

## ONE YEAR LATER

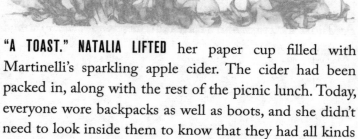

"A TOAST." NATALIA LIFTED her paper cup filled with Martinelli's sparkling apple cider. The cider had been packed in, along with the rest of the picnic lunch. Today, everyone wore backpacks as well as boots, and she didn't need to look inside them to know that they had all kinds of gear. A year after the hike that had almost cost them their lives, most of their little group was back where it had all begun. Back at Basin Falls.

The trail to the falls had reopened only two weeks ago. While the water and rocks looked the same as they had the year before, everything surrounding them was different. Many of the trees still stood, but their trunks were charred black as charcoal and missing all their lower branches. The forest floor, which last year had been lushly carpeted with ferns, was now bare except for a few small, bouncy green fronds.

Still, they were lucky to be able to be here. Due to the danger of rockfalls and landslides, the Forest Service had announced that many other trails, including Twisted and Cougar Creek, would not reopen for months or even years.

"A toast to Susan and AJ," Natalia continued.

"To Susan and AJ," people echoed as they raised their cups and then tipped them back. This was the first time all of them had seen each other since the hospital. It had felt important to gather today to mark the anniversary of their narrow escape.

Three of them were missing, but for different reasons. Susan was now living in an assisted-living facility. Natalia had visited her a few times, but on the last occasion it had been clear that the older woman didn't remember her. The only consolation had been that the facility also housed two cats and a golden retriever. Susan's daughter had told Natalia that her mom sometimes spent hours with the dog, petting and brushing it.

AJ was also absent. Right after the fire, he had joined a gym and then, three months ago, the navy.

And, of course, Jason wasn't with them. He was still sitting in jail awaiting trial. The museum guard had also been arrested. Their partner, Brian, had managed to evade the law. The other stolen jeweled items—a belt buckle, a hair clip, a necklace, a pair of earrings, and even shoe buckles—had never turned up. Because the pieces were so recognizable, it was feared that they had been broken down, the gems recut and the gold melted to render them sellable.

The jewelry wasn't the only thing that had undergone a transformation. Today it was strange for Natalia to think of her old self, the girl who had been in this exact same place a year ago. She had been so anxious at the beginning of that day, anxious about hiking, anxious about Wyatt, anxious about pretty much everything.

That single stretch of less than twenty-four hours in

the woods had changed her. Had changed them all, as far as she could tell.

After Wyatt had managed to catch Trask with the trekking pole, he and Lisa were able to hold on to Trask and get him back into the child carrier. At the same time, Marco had lashed himself to the handrail with Darryl's belt. On his back was the child carrier. Wyatt and Lisa managed to wrangle Trask inside. Then Wyatt had grabbed hold of the handrail with one hand and Natalia hand with the other. With him pulling, she had clambered to her feet and then immediately wrapped her arms around the handrail. With Wyatt's surefooted guidance, all of them had been able to get back to solid ground.

Once Wyatt and Natalia were on the other side, with Trask safe on his back, Wyatt gave her another hug and an even bigger kiss.

Then he gave Trask to Lisa, squared his shoulders, and went back across for Ryan and then Jason.

Once they were all across the bridge, the group somehow hiked the last three miles to the road, staggering forward powered by nothing more than sheer determination. Just before they reached it, Ryan's and Darryl's cell phones got service. First they called 9-1-1, then they passed the phones around so people could notify their families. By the time they clambered up the last bit of trail, paramedics, search and rescue volunteers, and a sheriff's deputy were just arriving.

The group's first stop was the hospital, which evaluated and treated their injuries. Natalia had two broken ribs, which she was told would heal on their own in about six weeks. Even Blue's scorched paws were salved and bandaged. As a precaution, Marco and Zion were kept overnight. Ryan spent two days in the hospital, but in the end didn't need skin grafts.

The ends of Jason's collarbone had been put back together, and his arm had been put in a sling. By the time Natalia left, officers from three different agencies were interviewing him.

Just before her parents picked her up, the emergency department doctor, a guy about her parents' age, sought her out.

"Everyone keeps telling me about how you took care of some big medical emergencies out there in the woods," he said. "This is what I do for a living, but I've got staff and supplies and even machines. You had nothing but a little first aid kit."

Natalia shrugged, embarrassed. "We all worked together. Once we knew no one was coming to rescue us, we realized *we* were the only ones who could save us."

It turned out their group hadn't been the only hikers trapped in the woods that day. To get people out, first responders had been forced to rely on sketchy information and a lot of unknowns. Everything had been on the move: dozens of stranded hikers, their would-be rescuers, and the fire itself. Some groups on other trails had also self-rescued, but unlike their group, they hadn't been trapped overnight. Forest Service rangers who happened to be nearby had walked two different groups of hikers out. And the Oregon National Guard had plucked three hikers off nearby Ransom Ridge with a Chinook helicopter.

Through some miracle, not one person died in the fire that day or the ones following. It took three months to be fully extinguished. By then, it had destroyed forty-eight thousand acres of wilderness and forced the evacuation of a dozen small towns. Interstate 84, which ran east to west, had been closed for weeks. Even now, a year after the fire, a lot of businesses along the corridor were still feeling the effects of months without income.

But it could have been so much worse. People had survived, structures had mostly survived, whole towns had survived. If the wind had pushed the fire west, it could have threatened Portland. As it was, the city had spent several months covered with a dusting of windblown ash. People had worn masks to exercise or even just go outside.

In addition to being charged with the museum's robbery, Jason was also facing eight counts of reckless burning, one count of criminal mischief, and one count of reckless endangerment of others.

"I can't believe he's pleading not guilty," Darryl said now.

Lisa replied like the lawyer it turned out she was. "It's pretty standard. If he's smart, he'll take a plea deal and not let it go to trial. Even if jurors say they're impartial, it's going to be hard to find twelve people who weren't affected in some way by the fire."

"Enough about Jason." Beatriz leaned forward. "I want to know how all you guys are doing. Like does Trask remember anything?"

They all turned to look at Trask. Farther down the shore, the two-year-old was throwing a stick for Blue with great enthusiasm and terrible aim and distance. Each time it landed only about five feet away. And each time Blue happily retrieved it and dropped it for Trask to throw again.

"He's never had a single nightmare." Lisa gave them a lopsided smile. "I can't say the same for us. But we're a lot better now."

Ryan held out his hands and flexed his fingers. "My burns have healed. Now I'm just working on range of motion."

"How about you guys, Beatriz?" Lisa asked.

Beatriz held out her own left hand. Her nails were silver and sparkly. And on the ring finger was a plain gold band topped with a tiny diamond. Marco grinned and put his arm around her.

"You're engaged!" Natalia exclaimed.

"Congratulations, you two!" Lisa said. "I think this calls for another toast."

"Zion, can you fill up everyone's cups?" Darryl asked. As his grandson picked up the bottle, he said, "And Zion and I are both doing well. We've got EpiPens stashed everyplace, and now I always carry a few packets of sugar. Just in case."

Zion spoke up. "Before we came here, we went to REI and got the ten essentials." He shot a shy, sidelong glance at Wyatt. "And I'm going to join Boy Scouts next year. I know their motto is 'Be Prepared.' Like you were."

Wyatt held out his hand so Zion could give him a high five, which he did with a grin.

"How about you, Wyatt? How did college go this year?" Darryl asked.

"I like engineering, but I'm still trying to figure out what kind of engineer I want to be."

"You should think about bridges," Darryl suggested. "You did pretty well with the bridge we had to cross."

Ryan looked over at Natalia. "And what about you?"

"I just got certified in wilderness medicine." The first day, they had gone around the room to say why they were taking the class. One person had sea kayaked. Another free rock climbed, which meant they did it with no ropes. Natalia had simply said she liked to hike, but then the rock climber looked at her more closely and said, "Aren't you one of the Basin Falls Twelve?" But hardly anyone had recognized her lately. Her fifteen minutes of fame had been up a long time ago.

The course instructors had done their best to make it feel real, including putting special makeup on people so they appeared to be bruised, bleeding, or badly infected. When faced with someone pretending to be screaming in pain, some of Natalia's classmates had panicked and forgotten everything they had just learned. For her, it had been a cakewalk.

Beatriz leaned forward. "Still planning on going into medicine?"

"First I have to get my undergrad degree. I'm going to major in biology."

"Where are you going?" Ryan asked.

"Uh, Columbia University." It still felt a little fantastic. "Part of the application is writing an essay. You can guess what I wrote about." After talking to Dr. Paris, Natalia had even included Conner's death.

Beatriz's eyes widened. "Columbia! We need another toast. Can you top us up, Zion?" She turned to Wyatt. "Are you going to go see Natalia when she's in the Big Apple?"

She was obviously trying to play matchmaker. But they were way ahead of her.

"Of course." As he spoke, Wyatt brushed his fingers against the top of Natalia's hand. When he was at school, they texted nearly every day. And when he was home, they spent most of their time together. This summer, they were both back at work at the Dairy Barn, where they occasionally snuck a kiss in the walk-in cooler.

"It sounds like we've got plenty to celebrate," Lisa said. "There were so many times a year ago when I would have said none of us was going to make it out."

Natalia said, "The one thing that makes me feel sad is how different everything is. On the drive out here, I was looking across the Columbia River into Washington. It makes it obvious how much we've lost." Before, the two sides of the river had been like mirrors of each other. Now instead of trees, the ridgeline on the Oregon side was topped with a long line of blackened, leafless trunks, like the bars of a cage.

Wyatt put his arm around her shoulders. "The Gorge is already starting over. She'll come back."

Natalia bit her lip. "But it won't be the same."

"Nothing ever is," he said simply. "But that doesn't mean it can't be just as good."

# A NOTE FROM THE AUTHOR

This book was inspired by the Eagle Creek Fire, which decimated the Columbia Gorge in 2017. A single person's careless actions endangered many lives and burned fifty thousand acres. Among those affected by the fire were a variety of people who had taken a short hike to a waterfall. Trapped by the fire, the group had to flee for their lives.

# ACKNOWLEDGMENTS

So many people helped me pull this book together. Any errors are my own.

Lee Etten, a fire captain and paramedic, Portland Fire & Rescue, explained how house fires behave.

Joe Collins, a firefighter and paramedic, helped me figure out the best way to torch a car—and how to make that fire spread.

Jake Keller, a volunteer with Multnomah County Search and Rescue, helped me brainstorm worst-case scenarios.

To help me write this book, I became certified in wilderness medicine through NOLS (which began life as the National Outdoor Leadership School). One of my instructors was Paul Dreyer, CEO of Avid4 Adventure (avid4.com), which introduces kids to the wonders of the outdoors. For months after the course ended, Paul answered a million and one questions about how to deal with various first aid emergencies in the wilderness.

Craig Aronson II, RN, helped me understand what would happen to a diabetic who hiked for hours and did not eat.

Ginny Gustin, president of Austin Babywearing, answered a bunch of bizarre questions from a stranger about how to carry a toddler in various dangerous scenarios.

Garrett Gustafson, a senior structural engineer for MaineDOT's Bridge Program, explained how bridges work and told me all the correct names for bridge parts.

Sheri Burns, honeybeesonline.com, answered my questions about wild bees nesting in trees.

Marco Carocari, a photographer and writer, bid in a fundraising auction to have his name used in this book. He even sent me pictures of himself when he was the same age as the fictional Marco.

Even I find it hard to believe, but this is my twenty-fifth book with my agent, Wendy Schmalz.

My editor, Christy Ottaviano, helped me ramp up the book's tension. Associate editor Jessica Anderson has a sharp eye and keeps us all organized. Publicist Morgan Rath has helped me survive planes, trains, and automobiles. Mike Burroughs designed the amazing cover. Other wonderful folks at Henry Holt include Nancee Adams, Melissa Croce, Lucy Del Priore, Molly Ellis, Alexei Esikoff, Erica Ferguson, Katie Halata, and Allison Verost.